CLUES

I CLU ES 0631862 K

P9-APW-500

copy 2

PB
J
ROMM
$6.95
11/25/85

ROMM, J. LEONARD
THE SWASTIKA ON THE
SYNAGOGUE DOOR

DATE DUE			

BETH ISRAEL LIBRARY
VINELAND, NJ 08360

BETH ISRAEL SYNAGOGUE LIBRARY

The Swastika on
the Synagogue Door

BETH ISRAEL SYNAGOGUE LIBRARY

The Swastika on the Synagogue Door

A Lazarus Family Mystery

J. Leonard Romm

Illustrated by
Kathleen F. Marks

ROSSEL BOOKS

Chappaqua, New York

© Copyright, 1984 by
J. Leonard Romm
Published by Rossel Books,
44 Dunbow Drive,
Chappaqua, New York 10514
(914) 238-8954

All rights reserved. No part of this book may be
reproduced or transmitted in any form or by any
means, electronic or mechanical, including pho-
tocopying, recording, or any information storage
or retrieval system without written permission
from the Publisher.

Library of Congress Cataloging in Publication Data

Romm, J. Leonard, 1946-
  The swastika on the synagogue door.

  (A Lazarus Family mystery)
  Summary: When a Long Island synagogue is defaced
with a swastika and an anti-Semitic slogan, a teenage
brother and sister try to solve the mystery with the help of
their rabbi and a Holocaust survivor.
  [1. Mystery and detective stories. 2. Jews—Fiction.
3. Prejudices—Fiction] I. Title. II. Series.
PZ7.R6615Sw 1984   [Fic]   83-27263
ISBN 0-940646-53-6 (pbk.)

Manufactured in the United States of America

To my wife Diane,
   who nurtures potentiali-
   ties within me I would
   not fulfill on my own;
To my son Zvi,
   my young colleague and
   teacher, perceptive beyond his years, whose
   judgments, opinions, and
   reactions I valued
   throughout this work;
To my son Gadi,
   whose playful wit and
   burning bright humor are
   both my delight and my
   inspiration;
To these three,
   without whom I am not
   whole;
I dedicate with love this gift
of my labor.

The Swastika on the Synagogue Door

1
The Yellow Camaro

Wednesday night. 11:02 P.M.

The '71 yellow Camaro peeled rubber and squealed a scream of panic as it roared out of a dark corner of the Belwyn Jewish Center parking lot. The parking lot was deserted but for a lone, late-model sedan. The neighbors sometimes left a car or two on synagogue property overnight.

The Camaro lurched into the circle of light cast on the parking lot by a Seaville Avenue streetlamp. Seaville Avenue, the main road, runs east-west through all of Belwyn, Long Island, and beyond through towns in both directions. The Belwyn Jewish Center's high-stepped front entrance with its enormous white pillars faces south onto Seaville Avenue. So does the entrance to its parking lot which is across a narrow side street just beyond the synagogue's eastern wall.

The yellow Camaro insanely banged into the right rear quarter panel of the parked sedan, careened left and right, then sped out the entrance of the lot. Whoever was driving gunned the motor and headed east down Seaville Avenue.

This strange accident might have gone unnoticed. But Mrs. Anderson, who lived in the small Cape Cod house across the street from the parking lot was sitting on her sofa looking out the bay window of her living room. She was nervous. Her son Keith had left the house right after dinner, saying he was going out with some friends. She didn't know who. Here it was—late—he was only fourteen; not back yet, and there was school tomorrow.

Seeing the accident, Mrs. Anderson thought for a moment about crossing the street and leaving a note on the windshield of the damaged sedan. Then she changed her mind. What could she say? She did not catch the license number of the yellow car. All she could remember about it was that it was festooned with many bumper stickers on its rear end, none of which she could read from where she was sitting. Besides, this hit-and-run was someone else's headache, someone else's insurance problem. It happened all the time.

Four blocks east down Seaville Avenue, in the section of Belwyn where the homes were larger, the lawns bigger and well-landscaped, sixteen-year-old Terri Lazarus looked up from her biology textbook with a start. A screech of brakes—without the thud of an accident—made her run to the front door and open it to see what was happening.

She was just in time to spy the yellow Camaro speeding off, going east down Seaville. Mr. Suschin, her neighbor across the street, was sitting in his big blue Oldsmobile. He was a study in suddenly-stopped motion—backed out of his driveway, halfway onto Seaville Avenue. As she watched, Mr. Suschin ver-r-ry slowly took his foot off the brake and backed the Oldsmobile into the street, then cautiously drove westward.

"A near miss," said Terri to her eighteen-year-old brother Robert.

She went back to the dining room table where Robert was helping her study for her big biology exam tomorrow. Her older brother was great at math and science. The rest of the family was already in bed for the night. Henkin always went to bed by ten. He had to get up early for morning *minyan.*

The two teens turned back to the work of cramming the internal parts of Rana *pipiens* into Terri's memory. They were glad that Henkin was asleep. Otherwise the old man would be right in the middle of their cram session, butting in with his well-meaning but befuddled "help." The only frogs he knew about, they agreed, were the ones that had plagued Pharaoh in Egypt.

Later, Officer Oates of the Nassau County Fifth Precinct remembered that he ticketed a '71 Camaro for running a red light at the corner of Seaville Avenue and Dakota Street at 11:10 P.M. that night. He remembered because it seemed unusual for a car registered to a Samuel *Epstein,* driven by a Brian *Epstein,* age eighteen, to be plastered with bumper stickers proclaiming "HONK, IF YOU LOVE JESUS," "JESUS IS THE LIFE AND THE RESURRECTION," "I AM BORN AGAIN," and the like.

"The way these kids drive," thought Officer Oates, "he'll have to be 'born again' at least twenty times just to live through his teens."

Officer Oates was starting to fill out a report form on his clipboard.

2
The Shock

Thursday morning. 6:15 A.M.

Henkin was the first to see it.

His eyes filled with tears—tears of rage, tears of memories deep inside that would hurt forever, tears of revenge never taken.

"The hands that did this thing should only fall off and be eaten by maggots," he said. That was all he could think to say in the moment he saw it.

Henkin was the first to arrive at the synagogue. Since his retirement five years ago, Henkin had become the unofficial *shammes* of the Belwyn Jewish Center. It was he who opened the doors for morning *minyan*. This morning, he was here five minutes early. Thursday was a Torah-reading day. Davening would begin a bit earlier. Some of the morning *minyan* regulars had to catch the Long Island Railroad.

As *shammes*, Henkin had the keys to the white, double-door side entrance to the synagogue, the entrance facing the parking lot. This door had become, long ago, the *de facto* main entrance to the shul. It led to a street-level hallway. The synagogue office and the rabbi's study were just to the left inside the entrance. The downstairs chapel, the place where weekday services were held, was to the immediate right.

Henkin was inwardly proud that being *shammes* entitled him to a copy of the key to the side entrance latch, the smaller key to the peripheral alarm system, and the large key to the synagogue office. He knew the several coded patterns of buttons to push in order to release and to set the photoelectric internal alarm system from the box on the left wall just inside the parking lot entrance to the synagogue.

The Belwyn Jewish Center was an electronic fortress standing firm against the burglaries that beset other houses of worship on Long Island. Henkin felt like the Keeper of the Gate.

So the shock was all the greater.

And Henkin was the first to see it.

On the big, white double-door of the parking-lot entrance was a three-foot square, ugly, spray-painted black SWASTIKA!

Over it, on the door, in fuzzy black-painted scrawl, were the words: KILL THE JEWS!

"Nazis. The world is filled with Nazis. May they all rot in Hell." It was the second thing Henkin could think to say.

Henkin went inside the synagogue, his heavy key ring still in his trembling hands. The rabbi would arrive in a few minutes. *He* would know what to do.

Henkin turned on the chapel lights. He fidgeted with the velvet cover on the reader's lectern, smoothing it and resmoothing it nervously. Finally, he sat down on the front pew and waited.

One by one the Thursday morning *minyan* "regulars" came into the chapel. Their faces were white with fear, anger, disgust, sadness, hatred. Every one clearly felt that the sanctity of *his* synagogue had been violated.

"A *shondeh!* Such a disgrace!"

"Imagine. Spray-painting a synagogue, a house of God!"

"And a swastika. And, 'Kill the Jews!' Sick minds."

"America. And in this day and age. Doesn't the world ever learn *anything?*"

"It's kids, thinking they're cute."

"You can't excuse kids."

"They get it from their homes. You think there's no more anti-Semitism left in Belwyn? I remember just before World War II: there was a Belwyn chapter of the German-American Bund. They used to hold parades, in Nazi uniforms, goose-stepping down Main Street."

"Aw, c'mon. There's nothing like that now. Don't be paranoid."

"Let's call the cops."

"What good will that do?"

"Plenty, if they catch the ones who did it. It's a crime to paint slogans on a synagogue."

"If I'd have caught them, I'd have broken their heads!"

"Then *you'd* get arrested. Better to call the police."

"So the cops catch them. They go to trial. They'll get a slap on the wrist, and be back out on the streets. Then, we'll have real *tzuris,* more trouble. They'll be back again and again, for spite—and do even worse."

"So, what should we do? Hide our heads in the sand?"

"We should have Johnny, the custodian, sandpaper the door and repaint it. Then, forget it! It's a nuisance, like the eggs they throw against the door on Halloween."

"No. First thing, we'll report it to the police. Then, let's daven. It's time for the morning prayers." The last voice was that of Rabbi Rosen, a young man near the age of thirty who looked even younger. In automatic respect for the rabbi's wishes, the cluster of upset, debating Jews became a *minyan* and turned their attention to praying, as much as they could.

While some of the regulars wrapped themselves in *tallit* and placed *tephillin* on head and arm, Rabbi Rosen went into the synagogue office across the hall and put in a call to the Fifth Precinct. He made a quick report. Then he returned to the chapel to join the service.

He wrapped himself in his long *tallit* and wound the straps of his *tephillin* around his arm and let them fall on either side of his head. Then he stood behind the rows of pews next to Robert Lazarus. Robert had come in while the rabbi was on the telephone. He looked shaken by his sight of the desecration.

The rabbi put his hand on Robert's shoulder, then picked up a prayer book from the rack on the back of the last pew. "That's partly why we daven, too. So that we don't become like the spray-painters."

Henkin led the service from the reader's lectern. His voice sounded different this morning. He was thinking about the swastika.

Usually, Henkin mumbled. This morning, his week-day chant sounded like it was coming through clenched teeth.

Also, Henkin raised his voice when he came to the Hebrew words, *"V'chol ha-rish'ah k'rega tovaid . . .,"* "And let evil perish speedily, and may all of God's enemies be quickly cut off, and may the wicked speedily be uprooted, crushed, and defeated."

Only Rabbi Rosen understood the full meaning of Henkin's raised voice. He and Henkin were the only two worshippers in the chapel who understood all the Hebrew of the morning prayer service.

10

There were fifteen regulars at that Thursday morning *minyan*. Five were old men like Henkin who were retirees and who came to every service, every single day of the year. Another six men were in their thirties, forties, and fifties. They were Thursday morning "recruits." They had pledged Thursday morning as their "*minyan* day." On the High Holy Days, Rabbi Rosen had asked people to pledge one morning each week for attending the *minyan*.

In addition to the men, there was a middle-aged woman who came to say the *Kaddish* prayer in memory of her husband who had died recently. She, too, was one of the regulars. The rabbi was there every day.

The remaining two were teenagers. One of them was Robert Lazarus who had pledged "Thursday mornings and any other time that Henkin could get him out of bed in time for synagogue."

Just being together in the morning *minyan* worked a friendly magic among this diverse group. This morning, however, they felt pulled together even more closely by their shared sense of shock, anger, and hurt—by the desecration of their shul.

Each, in his or her own way, offered a special prayer during the forty-minute service of rapid-fire Hebrew chanting and mumbled humming. Each, in his or her own way, felt really Jewish this morning.

As the minyan read the Psalm for Thursday, before the final *Kaddish,* Rabbi Rosen saw Officer Oates standing in the hallway, peering through the window of the chapel door. Six-foot-six, brawny, in a Nassau County policeman's uniform, complete with mirrored aviator sunglasses, Officer Oates contrasted sharply with the smaller men inside. Some of the men were hurriedly removing their *tephillin,* ready to hear what the rabbi would say to this earthly representative of truth, justice, and the American way.

Rabbi Rosen stood in the hallway, still wrapped in his *tallit* and *tephillin*. The headband of his *tephillin* hardly reached the policeman's upper sleeve insignia. The two were soon surrounded by those *minyanaires* who did not have to run to their cars, drive to the Belwyn railroad station, and make the 7:20 train to work in New York City.

"I'm answering your call," said Officer Oates. "It's a crying shame. Anything *else* painted anywhere around the building or inside it?"

"We didn't have a chance to look yet. We went ahead and started morning services," said the rabbi.

"Let's go see."

The rabbi led the small procession of worshippers and the tall policeman through all the inside corridors, into every room of the Belwyn Jewish Center. They trekked up the stairs to the main sanctuary, the ballroom, and the kitchen. They walked in a snaking line down the back stairwell to the boiler room, the storage room, the Hebrew School classrooms, and the library, until they reached the first floor chapel again. Everything seemed in order.

Meanwhile, Robert walked around the entire outside of the synagogue building. Only the side-entrance door had been touched. Robert joined the group, now standing outside the side door, and told them that the rest of the building was clean.

"They couldn't have gotten inside without tripping the alarm system which is wired to your precinct station," said Rabbi Rosen to the policeman. Officer Oates was starting to fill out a report form on his clipboard.

"We even hide our silver Torah ornaments all year long, and take them out just for the High Holy Days," put in Henkin. "Some world we live in."

"Is there anyone you might suspect?" asked Officer Oates, looking at his clipboard. "A fired employee? Janitor, perhaps?"

"Oh, no. Nothing like that. We did bawl Johnny out this week for slacking off and not filling the toilet paper dispensers in the ladies' room. The ladies at the sisterhood luncheon last Monday were awful rough on him. But, no. He's no suspect. He loves this place. He knows more about Jewish customs and dietary laws in the kitchen than half the Jews in the congregation. No. He can't be a suspect. I wouldn't even consider it," answered the rabbi.

Officer Oates just kept on writing.

The rest of the *minyan* people left for their cars, except for Robert, Henkin, and the rabbi. They remained, still talking with Officer Oates.

"It's not an easy thing to trace, since there are no witnesses. But we'll try to check it out."

"Thank you, Officer," said the rabbi.

As the policeman was about to cross the side street to where he had parked his patrol car on the synagogue's lot, a plump, forty-ish woman from the Cape Cod house across Seaville Avenue in a purple, flowered, double-knit housecoat and fuzzy, lavender bedroom slippers, with pink, plastic curlers in her hair, came running up to the foursome.

"I saw a car take off like a shot from here last night around eleven o'clock," she said, still panting from her run. "I think it was yellow. It hit that sedan over there."

Officer Oates wrote that down, too. He had been working overtime through the late night to the early morning shift. On his clipboard was still his copy of the summons for a yellow Camaro that had run a red light on Seaville Avenue late last night. He remembered *that* car. A Jewish kid with Jesus stickers.

"Did the car have a lot of bumper stickers?" asked the policeman.

"I think so. Yes, but I couldn't read them."

Robert Lazarus knew that car, too. He had seen it often enough in the student parking lot at Belwyn High. He made a quick note to himself. There were a few questions he would like to ask at school that day.

"I'll check it out," said Officer Oates. He got into his patrol car, said something into his radio microphone, and drove away.

"To do a thing like that," said Mrs. Anderson to the three who were standing and staring dejectedly at the side door blemished by that vicious symbol, "it's just a disgrace, a real disgrace." She crossed the avenue, and disappeared into her house.

"*Zachor es asher asa l'chaw Amolek,*" muttered Henkin. Robert looked at the rabbi.

"He's quoting the Torah," said Rabbi Rosen.

"*Zachor et asher asa l'cha Amalek,*" the rabbi requoted in his more Israeli-sounding Hebrew. "It means, 'Remember what Amalek did to you.' The people of Amalek attacked the defenseless among the Israelites in the wilderness. They attacked from the rear, by surprise, for no real reason. They were heartless, cruel, and now we think of them whenever anyone attacks the Jewish people for no cause other than meanness."

"*Zachor es asher asa l'chaw Amolek.*"
It was the third thing Henkin could think to say.

3

The Lazarus Household

"AR-R-R-O-O-OM. PSHEW-PSHEW-PSHEW!"

Jeff Lazarus watched the butter melt into the pockmarked surface of his English muffin. He held the muffin-half in his right hand, between his thumb and forefinger. He tilted his muffin to the left and to the right, pretending it was a spaceship dodging laser blasts.

"What are *you* doing?" Terri looked up at him, annoyed, from across the butcher-block breakfast table in the kitchen.

"Oh, nothing," countered Jeff, sheepishly.

"Well, *keep it* nothing. I have a biology exam today, nerd, and I'm studying."

Terri peered into the thick textbook open flat before her on the table, read something, then looked up with a faraway stare. She took a sip of cocoa, then quickly directed her eyes back to the textbook page.

"I'm *not* a nerd," thought Jeff to himself. He knew enough, at moments like these, not to say it out loud. No one messed with Terri while she was studying.

In his twelve years and three months on this earth, Jeff had accumulated a wealth of worldly information. He knew it all. Just ask him.

Jeff went back to studying his English muffin, a fit subject for deep thought before a day of classes and chaos at Belwyn Junior High.

He knew, for instance, that the store brand of English muffins were infinitely superior to the nationally advertised kind, though both were better than toast. Both muffin brands tasted roughly the same. But the national brand were *milchig*. The store brand were *pareve*. You could have the store brand at breakfast with butter, and also at dinner with hamburgers.

Jeff was silently pleased with himself. The day had not yet started and here he had already decided the case for "English muffins and the Jewish Question." He was a regular think-tank. Jeff was nobody's fool.

Terri looked up again and said something out loud, speaking to no one in particular.

"The cloaca of the female Rana *pipiens* is the external opening beyond the two ovisacs. In males, it is the opening beyond the two sperm sacs."

Jeff couldn't help himself. He perked up at the mention of "sperm sacs." His curiosity got the better of his judgment. Interrupting, he knew, was treading on thin ice with his older sister. Nevertheless, he did.

"Who the heck is Rana *pipiens?*"

"Not who, imbecile, *what!* Rana *pipiens* is the North American leopard frog. And I have to know the sucker inside out two hours from now. So, shut up and let me study."

"I know stuff about frogs," Jeff offered, tentatively.

"The only thing *you* know about frogs is how to run around camp chasing little girls with them." The Terri barometer was pointing toward "stormy weather ahead."

"That's not true. First of all, the only girls *I* know go around *catching* frogs at camp. They even beat the boys out for first string on the baseball teams. Hummungus *amazons*, that's what *they* are!"

"For crying out loud, Jeff. Will you stuff it?"

"In our science class last spring we had these tadpoles in a fishtank. We watched them change into frogs, see? It's called 'metamorphosis.' So there!"

Jeff felt as if he had won a victory.

Terri looked like she was ready to kill. She chose to ignore her little brother. "Ovary, oviduct, ovisac, *cloaca!* Got it!"

Terri turned on the caned kitchen chair. She strained to look through the kitchen doorway, past a corner of the dining room, out the front window of the living room to Seaville Avenue.

"I wish Robbie and Henkin would get back from *minyan* already. I want to get to school and get this test over with."

Jeff was still thinking about metamorphosis. He was wishing that *Terri* would change into something else.

Edmund Lazarus, their father, was out of town on business. He was often out of town on business. He bought and sold diamonds, internationally. This trip, he was not expected home until next Sunday.

Robert was allowed to use the family Buick whenever their father was away. All week long, Robert drove his sister and brother to school in the morning after breakfast. He dropped Jeff off at the junior high, and continued on to the high school both he and Terri attended.

After school, Jeff and Terri had to walk home.

Robert had a girlfriend.

And a car.

This morning he was a little late coming back from *minyan* with Henkin. Thursday morning *minyan* was always longer. They always had to rush to school after breakfast. This morning, the morning of Terri's biology exam, Robert was even later than usual.

Terri was getting nervous.

"How can he *do* this to me?" she pouted, chewing on a painted thumbnail. *Minyan* could be so inconvenient.

The Buick pulled into the driveway at the side of the Lazarus home.

Henkin slowly opened the passenger door. He swung his heavy shoes over the little plate on the door sill that advertised, "Body by Fisher." Then his feet touched the curb of the driveway. Henkin, frail in a baggy and old-fashioned suit, unfolded himself from the car seat like an aged inchworm straining for a higher twig on a tree branch.

He closed the car door behind him. It caught the latch but did not fully close. Henkin plodded across the lawn, one step at a time. Something was bothering him. Even Terri could see that.

Robert came around from the driver's side. He had slammed the door shut as though he were angry. He reached the front of the house well before Henkin, unlocking it with the housekey that was on the same ring as the car keys.

He waited for Henkin, held open the storm door and the house door for him, and followed the old man into the house.

"It sure took you long enough," complained Terri. "Remember? I've got a biology exam this morning."

"Terri," Robert said in a low voice, "something happened at the temple."

"Something's always happening at the temple. So what?"

"No. I mean something really awful. It still makes me sick to think about it," continued Robert.

"What happened?" asked Jeff, as he joined them in the living room.

"Some Nazi bastards painted a big swastika on the shul door," spit Henkin in a tone of voice they had never heard from him before.

The two younger Lazaruses were as startled by Henkin's voice as they were by the news.

Everyone was suddenly quiet, glancing from one to the other.

They had come to see Henkin as another parent in their home—maybe as an extra grandfather. All four of their real grandparents were still living, but their father's parents were in Florida in an adult retirement community, and their mother's parents were all in the Boston area. They saw them from time to time, like at Passover and at school vacations. But Henkin, as crotchety as he was, as nagging as he could be when it came to things Jewish, was now a part of the family.

In his own strange way, and differently from each of the Lazarus children, Henkin was also a part of their hearts.

When their mother was killed in an automobile accident two years ago, their father and Robert had gone to *minyan* every day of the week for eleven months to say *Kaddish*. They got to know Henkin up close, as he led and bullied the unique, ever-changing confederation of *minyan* regulars.

The Lazarus family had suffered a great loss with the death of Ruth Lazarus. She had been central to their family, holding them together, especially when their father was away so often on business. In fact, for one entire year, their father had not traveled at all. That, in itself, was a great tribute to Ruth Lazarus.

Henkin lost his wife Tillie about the same time. The couple had never had any children of their own, so far as the Lazarus family or anyone in Belwyn knew. But for thirty years Henkin and Tillie had lived in Belwyn.

People who shared the morning prayers tended to get close—and especially those who shared sadnesses.

One month after Ruth Lazarus's death, after her sister Louise left to return to Boston, Edmund Lazarus struck a deal with Henkin at morning *minyan*.

Henkin could use a family and companionship.

Edmund needed someone to tend house, to cook meals, and to watch over the children while he went on business.

Henkin would receive free room and board in the large Lazarus house. A first-floor room was fixed up for him. It had once been the children's play room. And it was next to the first-floor bath.

The Lazarus children got Henkin.

Some might think it crazy to bring an elderly stranger into a house full of children. Nonetheless, Henkin moved in.

Henkin kept the house a home.

A Jewish home.

Henkin had become family.

"A swastika! I don't believe it," said Terri at last.

"And 'KILL THE JEWS!' painted above it," added Robert.

"What did you do?" asked Jeff.

The rabbi called the cops. A big cop came and asked questions."

"Any suspects?" asked Jeff, feeling a little like a television detective.

"The lady across the street saw a yellow car speed out of the parking lot last night. The cop seemed to know it. He asked her if it had a lot of bumper stickers."

Terri caught Robert's eye. She knew what he was thinking. "That weirdo Jesus-freak, Brian Epstein."

Robert nodded. "I'm going to see if I can find him at school today."

"Be careful, Robbie. You're not the police," said Terri.

"I just want to talk to him."

"He might just try to love-bomb you."

"Yeah. That's why he just might talk. Spray-painting a temple. Some love."

"Maybe he didn't do it," chipped in Jeff. "It doesn't sound right. A *Jesus*-freak painting swastikas?"

"He's a mixed-up kid," said Robert. "Who knows what he might do?"

"I'm on the school newspaper," Terri said. "It might just be a chance for some real investigative reporting."

"I don't think the Jesus-freak did it," decided Jeff, out loud.

"What do *you* know, anyway?" Terri said, glowering at Jeff. "Oh, my God. School! I've got a biology exam today."

"We know," said Jeff, looking at Robert.

"With all this swastika excitement, I'll forget everything I know about Rana *pipiens*. I'm going to flunk!"

"You always say that," said Jeff, "and you always get an A. I wish *I* could flunk the way you do."

"C'mon. Let's get in the car already," said Terri. She grabbed her school books.

Robert took his bookbag from the living room chair and followed her.

Jeff went back to the kitchen to get his books.

He saw Henkin standing at the kitchen counter by the sink, slicing a tomato with a big knife. Henkin was making wafer-thin slices in quick strokes, frowning like the tomato was his enemy.

Henkin always had prune juice, a salad, and a hard-boiled egg for weekday breakfast. A strange man.

"You look like that knife commercial on T.V.," said Jeff, smiling, as he grabbed his books.

"What?" Henkin looked up at him in a daze.

"*You* know. The one where the guy smashes a tomato with his hand and says, 'You can't slice a tomato with a karate chop'?"

"Ha-a-ah?"

"Skip it. See you this afternoon!" Jeff ran out the door toward the family car.

Henkin heard the motor start up and listened as the kids drove away to school.

He looked at the tomato half on the cutting board, the half he had not yet sliced.

He put down the knife.

He looked again at the tomato half as if he expected it to get up and laugh.

He made a fist with his wrinkled right hand. Jewish karate.

He smashed his fist down upon the tomato.

It splattered all over the counter top, dripping red tomato blood on his white shirt. Tomato drips made wet red *tzitzis*-like fringes down the side of the cabinet to the brick tile kitchen floor.

Henkin began to cry.

4
Thursday Happenings

Thursday. 9:05 A.M.

Rabbi Rosen sat in his study at the Belwyn Jewish Center. He looked up from the large leather-bound book of the Talmud and glanced at the wall clock across the room from his cluttered desk.

"B.B. should be in his store by now," he thought.

The rabbi jockeyed himself in his swivel chair and reached for the pushbutton phone. He lifted the receiver from its cradle, pressed the button marked "Local Calls," and played a tune with the pushbuttons that by now he knew by heart. Rabbi Rosen heard three distant-sounding rings. The store was just a few miles away.

A familiar female voice answered. "Braverman's Better Beds and Bedroom Furnishings."

"Mr. Braverman, please."

"Whom shall I say is calling, please?"

"Rabbi Rosen."

"Oh, Rabbi Rosen. I didn't recognize your voice what with all the excitement around here this morning. I'll see if B.B. can come to the phone."

Bernard B. Braverman was the current president of the Belwyn Jewish Center. He was fifty years old, self-made, a bear of a man in the bed business. He never looked like he got enough sleep. Being synagogue president for a year and a half didn't help.

He liked to be called B. B. "Not a big shot," he would tell people with a hearty laugh, "just a little shot."

B. B. came to the phone.

"Rabbi," he said. "I don't believe it. I just opened the store a minute ago. A guy was standing on the sidewalk, waiting to get in. So I let him in. He says he wants to buy a waterbed. So I show him a waterbed. He lies down on the waterbed to try it. People do that every day. Day in, day out. So, who notices that this guy's a mechanic. Who sees that he's got a screwdriver in his back pocket? Two seconds. *Two seconds!* That's all it took.

"Rabbi, do you know what happens when you puncture a waterbed? I've got water all over my showroom! Nine o'clock in the morning, and we're bailing out a flood! A sunken bedroom. And the carpeting? Saxony plush. Twenty dollars a square yard. Have you ever seen a soggy Saxony?"

"No, but the roof still leaks a little at the parsonage. I know what my living room carpet looks like wet," suggested the rabbi, hinting that the roof really could use a little fixing, and since it belonged to the synagogue . . .

"Didn't the House Committee fix your roof yet? I'll make a note to tell them again. Hold on a minute, Rabbi. *Alphonse, for God's sake, will you move the arc lamp?* Unplug it! God, we're going to short out all the electricity in this place. Mildred, see that Alphonse gets the water vacuum from the storage room. *Hurry!*

24

Oh, Rabbi, I'm up to my garters here in water. Can I call you back?"

"Well, it's important. It'll take a second. Something happened at the shul overnight," said the rabbi, choosing his words quickly.

"Just what I need," said B. B. "How much will it cost?"

"No. This is serious. Someone painted a swastika and the words 'Kill the Jews!' on the side entrance."

"Just what I need this morning. Just what I need."

The rabbi went on. "I called the Fifth Precinct and the police sent out a man. He came just after morning *minyan*."

"Now what?"

"I'd like to call *Newsday* and let them do a story."

"Is that wise, Rabbi? That kind of publicity might bring more trouble."

"I know. It's taking a risk. But the Jewish organizations advise not to keep quiet. In the past few years, other Long Island synagogues—even some private homes—have had similar occurrences. The more that it becomes public, perhaps the more we can *do* something about it."

"Do what you think is best, Rabbi. I'll back you one hundred percent."

"Thanks, B. B."

"Wait. Don't we have a Bar Mitzvah coming up this *Shabbos*? Shouldn't Johnny clean off the door in a hurry?"

"I think I'd like to leave it up over *Shabbat*," said the rabbi. "Our people should know what's going on and feel the shock. Very few of them come to morning services on the weekdays, but a lot of them will be here for the Bar Mitzvah."

"Well, I'll leave that to your judgment, Rabbi. Now, excuse me, I've got to run. The water has reached my telephone desk. Oh, God, no! Not the crushed velvet convertible sofa!"

Click.

Rabbi Rosen leaned back in his swivel chair and reached for the Nassau County phone book. He called *Newsday*.

9:40 A.M.

Terri Lazarus and her friend Mary Beth Brady hurried along a hallway of the Belwyn Senior High School. They were headed to biology class. Both girls carried a stack of textbooks on top of their looseleaf binders, cradled in their arms in front of them.

Terri's biology textbook was open on the top of her stack. She was walking, talking, and still studying— all at the same time.

A steady stream of students moved along with them, pushing them, sometimes passing them. Another steady stream moved in the opposite direction, at times jostling them. From behind, Terri and Mary Beth looked like two female forklifts, their designer logos swaying in unison on the back pockets of their jeans.

"Let's see: fat bodies, testes, sperm ducts, kidneys, renal ducts, sperm sacs, cloaca. Is that right?" Terri was still memorizing out loud.

"Look, it's close enough," said Mary Beth, rolling her eyes in exasperation. "An hour from now, who'll care?"

"I'm going to fail this one. I just know I'm going to fail."

"Do I have to hear this again? You always say it before every exam. And you always screw up the curve for everyone else by getting everything right. I bet you'll get the highest grade in the class."

"This time, I mean it. I've got a lot on my mind."

"Some cute boy? Well, don't wait for him to ask. You ask *him* out. Who is it?"

"Nothing like that. The boys in this school are all jerks."

"The Jewish boys, maybe. But, how about Tommy Patterson?"

"Sure. Both Henkin and Robbie would bust about ten guts apiece."

"It's your life, not theirs. What's Henkin got to say about it, anyway? He's not your father. You want to grow up to be a Henkin?"

"Leave Henkin alone, okay? He's all right. You just have to get to know him."

"Whatever you say. Look, *I've* gone out with *Jewish* boys. *My* parents don't care."

"Can we drop it? It's not a boy that's on my mind."

"Then, you can't have anything very important on your mind, after all."

"Just because all you think about is boys doesn't mean that everyone is like that. Last night, somebody painted a swastika on our synagogue. Robbie saw it this morning before school."

"That *is* gross. But, look, it's probably some kids playing a joke. You should see the graffiti on the back door of our church. You know what someone actually wrote?" asked Mary Beth with a giggle. She looked around. "I don't want to say it too loud."

"A swastika is different," Terri went on, paying no attention. "It's a big one. And they wrote, 'Kill the Jews!' above it. I saw it, too. Robbie drove past the synagogue on the way to school."

"You can't really think someone wants to kill the Jews. It's somebody's idea of a joke, that's all."

"Henkin saw it this morning, too. Before we left for school he looked really upset. I'm worried about him."

"How could you tell? Henkin *always* looks upset about something, doesn't he?"

"You'll never understand Henkin," said Terri. "You and I share so many things that you're like my sister. But you'll never understand Henkin."

"You're probaby right. But I do care about *you*. There's no use worrying about something you can't do anything about. We've got a test to take. And here we are. Let's go in and get good seats. I hope I can pull at least an 80."

"Good luck with Rana *pipiens!*" Terri said.

"With what?"

"Rana *pipiens.* Mary Beth, the whole test is on Rana *pipiens.*"

"I thought it was about a frog."

The biology test was multiple choice. Mr. Rosetti always gave five choices of answers per question. At least two of the answers for each question were obviously ridiculous. Rosetti had a sense of humor. He also tried to weight the odds on an exam in favor of the class's doing well. It was an honors course. He wanted to make sure it would look like one in the records.

There were twenty-five frog questions on the exam. Terri breezed through twenty, knowing the right answers even without the multiple choice. She was stuck on five of them. She discarded the answers she thought were obviously wrong, then picked the one that seemed to fit best.

All the time, it bothered her. If she got all five wrong, she would get an 80 on the test. Maybe Mary Beth would be happy with an 80, but it would pull Terri's average down a lot. Terri was biting her thumbnail again, purple polish and all. She thought, "If I get an 80, and do well the rest of the term on other exams, maybe Mr. Rosetti won't count the 80 into my average." He sometimes dropped the lowest test score in a term. "I'm upset. I'm thinking about that swastika. It's not fair. That's why I messed up this test."

The bell rang.

The test papers were collected.

Terri and Mary Beth left the classroom together. Christine Mobley and some other girls were waiting for them right outside the door.

"How'd you do?" Christine asked Mary Beth.

"I think I passed," said Mary Beth cheerfully.

"Terri I don't have to ask. You got a hundred, I'll bet," said Christine.

"I really messed up on this one," said Terri, depressed. "We'll see you later. We have to rush."

Terri and Mary Beth walked down the hall out of earshot of the other girls.

"Jews," said Christine, looking after the pair. "She's always belly-aching, and still she gets all the honors and awards. I don't know how Mary Beth can *stand* to hang out with her. Maybe she thinks that the Jewish smarts can rub off."

Terri and Mary Beth were hurrying to honors English together. They both liked English much better than biology. The class was reading Shakespeare's play, *The Merchant of Venice*. Mr. Goldberg acted out the parts. He spoke Shylock's lines in Elizabethan English with an imitation Yiddish accent.

It got a lot of laughs.

Noon.

Robert Lazarus took the brown paper bag containing his lunch from the top shelf of his locker, closed the door, and twisted the dial to lock his combination padlock. He looked inside the bag. Tuna fish. Again? The smell of the fish came up at him. It seemed that tuna fish sandwiches were the staff of life for the kosher-keeping Jew.

Since Henkin lived with them, all three Lazarus children had given in to the fact of life that they would be keeping the dietary laws more strictly than ever. Henkin cajoled them and badgered them. The Lazarus home had always been more or less kosher when their mother was alive, but the family ate non-kosher food when they went out to restaurants or in the school cafeteria.

Henkin changed that. He became the family *mashgiah*, the supervisor of *kashrut*. He did all the cooking. He watched over the movement of every plate, every fork, knife, and spoon in the kitchen as if he were a Brinks guard keeping an eye on money.

Now, when Robert opened a kitchen drawer— whether or not Henkin was in the house—he could hear Henkin's voice in his head, saying, *"Milchig, milchig!"* or *"Fleishig,* Robert, *fleishig!"*

Henkin had put an end to buying lunch in the school cafeterias. He rose up at five in the morning, every morning on school days, to make lunches for each of the three children before he went to morning *minyan.*

Jeff and Robert had given in totally. Terri still cheated now and then when she went out with her friends to the Belwyn burger hangouts. But even for Terri, ordering non-kosher food was getting harder all the time. Lately, she was settling just for a Coke and fries. Henkin had a way about him.

Robert and his lunch bag made their way to the high school dining hall.

Robert was looking for Brian Epstein, Jew-for-Jesus Epstein, to see if he could find out anything about what went on last night. Robert thought to himself, "It's ironic. Since Brian became a Jew for Jesus, he and I are among the few kids in all Belwyn High who keep *kosher!*"

Brian was sitting in a far corner of the cafeteria at the end of a long table near the wall. Only one other student was at the table, a Jewish kid named Seth Marder. Brian seemed to be talking nonstop to Seth as Robert came up to them.

Brian was speaking rapidly, waving half of a peanut butter and jelly sandwich enthusiastically to the rhythm of the points he was making.

"What we believe is *not* that man became God. Just the opposite. God became *man* so He could show His love toward us. You *do* believe God is great enough to do anything He wants. Why shouldn't He become man?"

Poor Seth looked sorry that he was sitting at this table. He wasn't getting to eat much lunch. He kept looking around to see if there were seats at any other table. He felt trapped into a discussion he didn't particularly want. But he was too polite to leave without some good excuse.

There didn't seem to be any. So Seth tried to answer as best he could. "Uh, gee. I don't know. I guess so. An all-powerful God *could* do anything He wanted. But to *say* that doesn't prove that God actually *did* it. Look, you could pick anything in the world and say a God who could do anything, could do that. It doesn't prove God actually did it. Say, to show His love for marine mammals, God became a *porpoise*. God is powerful enough to do that, isn't He? And porpoises, they say, are nearly as smart as human beings. Why not a porpoise?"

Brian waved his half-sandwich. Now there was a bite taken out of it. "Because Holy Scriptures are God's word and . . ."

But Seth was just warming up. He was on the offensive now, and he wanted to keep pushing. "Scientists say porpoises can communicate with each other. They have a language. Maybe they have their *own* Holy Scriptures. Maybe some porpoises think that God came down to the sea as a porpoise. Maybe they say *that* porpoise died in the coral reefs for the sins of all porpoises. After all, porpoises just kind of play and look happy. Porpoises don't seem to fight any wars or want to rule any kingdoms. Maybe the porpoise Messiah has *already* come. Maybe, being human is porpoise Hell. If you don't accept the porpoise Messiah as God, maybe after you die your punishment is to come back as a *human*. Maybe there are *Jewish* porpoises who don't believe God would become a porpoise at all: that God is God and porpoises are porpoises. Maybe Jewish porpoises just want to eat their lunch and not be . . ."

Robert Lazarus interrupted. "Hi, Seth. Could you excuse us? I'd like to talk to Brian privately for a minute."

"Uh, sure, Robbie," said Seth. He breathed a small sigh of relief, picked up his lunch tray, and a second later was seated five tables away. Safe.

"Robbie Lazarus. To what do I owe this honor? You haven't talked to me since Bar Mitzvah class at Belwyn Jewish Center."

"Has it been five years? I guess so. Maybe because I *kept* coming to temple and I didn't see you around to talk to you."

"Remember Bar Mitzvah class? We were the only two kids that year that learned Torah *trope* so that we could chant the Torah reading at our ceremonies."

"Yeah. I remember."

"Remember that old guy, Henkin? Boy, did he ever get angry when you didn't sing it exactly right. Does he still do the Bar Mitzvah training?"

"Yes, he does. In fact, Henkin lives with my family now. He's really pretty smart. We just didn't appreciate him then. You could learn a lot from him."

"Sure. How come he lives with you?"

"Since my mother died, he kind of keeps house for us."

"Yeah. I heard about your mother. It's a shame she wasn't saved."

Robert was both startled and confused by this.

"Well, the doctors did all they could. It was a pretty bad accident."

"No. I mean *saved*! Take a look at Romans, chapter

6, verse 23. Only by faith in Jesus is there eternal life. Without Jesus, you die without being saved."

Robert was beginning to become annoyed. It seemed stupid of Brian to tell him that there was something wrong with his *mother*, of all people. He held his anger down. Brian was quite a talker since he became a Jew for Jesus; and Robert was counting on this habit of talking out. He hoped to get some idea of what happened last night, or even to trip Brian into making a confession. So he was willing to bide his time. And, besides, he personally found Brian to be warped enough to be a curiosity.

"You know, Robbie," Brian went on, not even realizing he had insulted the memory of Ruth Lazarus in Robert's eyes, "you should come with me to *my* synagogue some time. Everyone there keeps the Sabbath and keeps the dietary laws. That's more than you could ever say about the Belwyn Jewish Center. You'd like our synagogue. You're religious, just like I am. And all the people at my synagogue are young; and we're all learning Hebrew and praying and studying Bible. The true way. Someone like you would really enjoy it."

"I like the Belwyn Center well enough. A lot of people our age are interested in it, now. We have a really nice rabbi who came a couple of years ago, and he's done a lot. Some of us kids even go to morning *minyan*."

"Ah, yes. The Belwyn Jewish Center. Dues have to be paid. And there's so much hypocrisy—people saying how much they love Judaism, but not practicing any of it. I never found what I was looking for there."

"I don't think you gave it much of a chance," Robert answered. "Doesn't your synagogue ask for dues? How does it support itself?"

"By free-will offerings. We each give what we can. No one has ever *asked* me for money."

"No one has ever asked me for money at the Belwyn Center. I'll bet your synagogue gets money from *outside*. It must. Anyway, lots of good things go on at the B.J.C. What you call hypocrisy is probably true of *any* group of people. But the Center is a good place."

"Well, my parents were never good Jews. They never observed anything. At my new synagogue the people practice Judaism according to the law—Orthodox. And they care about *me*."

"But, Brian, they believe in *Jesus*! You can't believe in Jesus and still be Jewish. It's a contradiction. If Christians observe *Shabbat* and keep kosher, it doesn't make them Jewish. It just makes them Christians who act like Jews."

"Everyone in my synagogue is Jewish. We have become *complete* Jews by accepting Jesus as our Savior."

"This has to be a long discussion. I don't even know if I have all the answers. You should talk to Henkin. I just know that Jesus is no completion for Jews. Believing in Jesus is a little like walking up a dead end street—it just doesn't go anywhere. If Christians want to believe it, that's one thing. For Jews, Jesus doesn't add anything. We're a completely different kind of religion. Your synagogue is not a synagogue, no matter what you call it. It's some strange, mixed-up cult. Why don't you try the Center again, now that you observe more Jewish laws? It's time to be *really* Jewish; not the kind of game that you're playing."

"I haven't been near the Belwyn Jewish Center in five years . . ." Brian began.

"That's not true. You were there last night."

Brian's whole body seemed to stiffen for a moment. He turned pale.

"What do you mean?"

"Your yellow Camaro. A witness described your car. It could only be yours—she remembered it down to the bumper stickers. The police wrote it down in their report."

"The police? What do the police have to do with it? Is it a crime to be in the parking lot of the great Belwyn Jewish Center?"

"I thought you said you *weren't* there for five years?"

"O.K., I'll level with you. I was in the parking lot last night. What's that got to do with the police?"

"Don't you know?"

"No. I got a ticket last night after leaving the parking lot. My dad was really sore at me this morning. We don't get along, even under the best of circumstances. But I'll pay the ticket. What more can the cops want?"

"Don't you know?"

"Uh, no." Brian shifted in his chair. "Tell me."

"The same cop who gave you the ticket last night was at the temple this morning. Someone spraypainted a big black swastika on the parking-lot entrance to the Center. You, my friend, are the prime suspect."

Brian lowered his head.

"Robbie, I didn't do it. It was there when I got there. Why should I paint a swastika on a synagogue? I'm a Jew myself. It would be a crime against Jesus."

"What made you leave in such a hurry? There was a witness. And why didn't you report it, if you saw it?"

"I can't tell you. But *I* didn't do it."

"Well, pretty soon you'll have to have a good story for the police. I promise you that. The rabbi and the congregation will get to the bottom of this. And so will I!"

"Jesus will protect me. He'll be my witness."

"He'll *have* to, Brian. Unless you tell what you know."

The bell rang. Lunch was over.

2:00 P.M.

"I don't see what a swastika on a synagogue has to do with the school newspaper," Ms. Feingold said. Ms.

Feingold was the faculty advisor of the Journalism Club, and she was speaking to Terri Lazarus. "Your assignment is to cover the Junior Prom."

"But, Ms. Feingold," pleaded Terri, astonished by the teacher's cold reaction to the idea, "this story could be the biggest ever in the B.H.S. *Blast's* history!"

"It's not a *school* story. It is of no interest to our readers. It doesn't belong in the school newspaper."

"Well, the synagogue is in Belwyn. It's only two miles away from the high school. Lots of kids at school belong to it."

"You could write something for your synagogue bulletin. But I don't see what you could write for the newspaper. A paragraph reporting some vandalism at a synagogue? Churches get robbed and vandalized, too. All the time. Should we put *every* story in the school newspaper? It would have to be that way to be fair to most of our readers. Most of them are not Jewish. But then we wouldn't have any room for school news."

"But a swastika and 'Kill the Jews!' is different from other kinds of vandalism. What if it turns out that one of the students in our school is the one who painted it?"

"You would have to have very good proof before we ever dared to print anything like an accusation. A school newspaper prints stories about students getting awards, or things going on in the school. It doesn't print accusations. Besides, by the time an accusation like that would be proven, everyone would be reading about it in the community newspapers. So we wouldn't be adding anything by printing it in the *Blast*."

"What about the angle of prejudice? There's lots of prejudice right here among the students at school. We could study prejudice in the story and how to overcome it."

"Jews aren't the only victims of prejudice. What about Blacks, Hispanics, American Indians . . . women? Why not write about the Women's Movement at school?"

"But the synagogue incident just happened! It's news! And I could use it as a starting point to explore all kinds of prejudice."

"Well, if you're really that set on it, give it a try. But see that it is a piece on prejudice. It has to be balanced. It has to be interesting to everyone."

"Thank you, Ms. Feingold."

"Remember, Terri," said Ms. Feingold. "Don't make it too Jewish."

2:30 P.M.

For Jeff Lazarus—and for every kid at the Belwyn Junior High—there were two places of peril at school. One was the students' bathroom, boys' and girls'. The other was the dark belly of the school, where the student lockers lined the basement corridors.

No one at Belwyn Junior High ever actually went to the bathroom in order "to go to the bathroom." No one in his right mind.

Bathrooms were headquarters for the tough kids who belonged to gangs. Bathrooms were for smoking, tobacco or pot, or both. Bathrooms were for drinking liquor. Bathrooms were for dealing—practically anything illegal could be bought or sold there. Bathrooms were dangerous.

Students like Jeff Lazarus—the majority of students—learned early in their days at the junior high how to hold their bodily functions in check for the entire school day. They never set foot in a school bathroom. If you survived the students hanging out in them, you could still get in trouble by being caught during one of the faculty's disciplinary raids. How could you prove that you were really there to go to the bathroom?

Jeff simply did not go to the bathroom at school. But he did have to go to his locker from time to time during the day. That was a risk that everyone had to take.

Jeff had to go to his locker now. It was the end of

the school day and he needed to get his Belwyn jacket and some books he wanted for homework.

Out of the corner of his eye he saw Keith Anderson and four other tough boys, all dressed and hair-styled like "dirts." They watched him as he went into the alcove leading to his locker.

Jeff was taking his jacket off the hook and grabbing his paperback Bar Mitzvah Maftir booklet off the shelf for his after-school lesson with Henkin, when he heard what he was hoping with all his might *not* to hear.

"Hello, Little Jeffrey. How is little Jeffrey today?" It was the voice of Keith Anderson. He was trying to sound friendly, in a mocking way. But he sounded menacing.

"Hi, Keith," said Jeff quickly. He turned in time to see Keith and the four grinning cohorts block his only escape route. Jeff quickly closed his locker door and clicked his padlock shut in the latch. He fumbled clumsily, his jacket in one hand and his school books in the other.

Keith's eyes narrowed and focused on the Maftir booklet, the top of the pile under Jeff's arm.

"What's that? *Heeb*-brew?"

"It's something I need to study for my Bar Mitzvah lessons." Jeff looked around, but there was no way out. He felt his heart beating fast.

One of the boys was palming and puffing a marijuana joint. At least two of Keith's gang were really high school age, but they kept getting left back. They were marking time until they could drop out of school legally. They looked on with sadistic anticipation, waiting to have some fun at the expense of Little Jeffrey. Keith was in charge. He was a full head taller than Jeff.

"We want some Bar Mitzvah lessons, too. Don't we? You get a lot of money for Bar Mitzvahs, don't you?"

While Keith turned his head dramatically, as though he were talking with his friends, his hand snatched the Maftir booklet from under Jeff's helpless arm.

"Let's see here," continued Keith. "Is this upside down, or do the pages go backwards? Hey, guys. Look at this picture with the kid. His arm is all tied up!"

"Keith," said Jeff, pleading. "It's kind of like a Bible."

"We just want to take lessons, too," said Keith calmly. He began to pull pages off the staples of the booklet and handed one to each of his friends.

Jeff could take it no longer. At the sight of his Maftir booklet being torn apart, he dropped his jacket and books. Without thinking, he kicked Keith in the groin.

Keith doubled over in pain. The rest of the Maftir booklet fell from his hands to the floor. The other boys crumpled the pages they held and tossed them at Jeff. In an instant, they surrounded him. He was slammed against his closed locker door. His legs gave out from under him, and he slumped to the floor. They kicked at his body, as he rolled into a ball to protect himself. As they kicked, they jeered at him, "Dirty, sneaky Jew-boy!"

Jeff was lucky. A teacher, alerted first by the smell of marijuana smoke and then by the noise, came down the stairs into the locker room.

One of the toughs saw the teacher come around the corner of the lockers and called to his friends. The four that had been kicking Jeff were gone in a moment. All the teacher ever saw was the fifth kid, limping a little, as he ran through the rows of lockers well ahead of the oncoming adult.

The teacher stopped as he came up to Jeff who was still lying bruised and stunned on the floor in a rubble of jacket, scattered schoolbooks, and crumpled Hebrew pages. Jeff was beyond crying. He just looked up at the face of the sympathetic teacher.

"Will you tell me who did it?" the teacher asked, helping Jeff to his feet, and picking up some of Jeff's scattered belongings.

"It doesn't matter," said Jeff.

"Okay," the teacher said, used to this answer, "but come with me. We'll see if the school nurse is still here."

3:30 P.M.

Rabbi Rosen and the *Newsday* reporter walked out the side door of the Belwyn Jewish Center, headed for the parking lot where the reporter had left his car parked. They turned once again to look at the swastika.

"I don't believe there is *much* anti-Semitism in Belwyn," said Rabbi Rosen. "Be sure you make *that* clear in your article."

5
Henkin's Heroics

Henkin turned the key, opening the front door of the Lazarus house on Seaville Avenue. He shuffled into the vestibule. He was worried.

Jeff had not shown up for Bar Mitzvah class at the shul. It was not like Jeff just not to show up for a lesson. For all of Jeff's wise-guy humor and childish pranks, Henkin knew that Jeff was a responsible kid, a good kid.

Henkin tried out several answers in his mind. Had something happened to Jeff on the way home from school? A car hit him? God forbid! No, someone would have called Henkin. Jeff had a wallet with an emergency card in his pocket.

Perhaps Jeff had been kidnapped. That kind of thing was in the newspapers all the time. Henkin thought to himself: "What would I do if he were kidnapped?" He ran through plans in his mind. What a tragedy! What a calamity! He was responsible for the children. Their father was out of town.

By the time he reached the vestibule, he knew what he had to do. Go to the kitchen phone. Call the Fifth Precinct.

Henkin plodded, one heavy step after another,

moving diagonally across the living room carpet, passing through a corner of the dining room, making his way to the kitchen, to the wall phone by the breakfast table. He reached for the Nassau County telephone book in his most troubled, arthritic manner.

Then he heard the noise.

"SHOUP, SHOUP, SHOUP-PAH-KE-E-EW!

"SHOUP, SHOUP, SHOUP-PAH-KE-E-EW!"

It was coming from a back room of the house.

Henkin put the telephone book down on the kitchen table. Someone was in the house. Doing what, Henkin could not imagine.

Should he call the police while he was still sitting by the telephone? Or should he go himself to investigate? Henkin was not a coward.

"SHOUP, SHOUP, SHOUP, SHOUP, SHOUP.

"PAH-KE-E-E-EW!"

Henkin cautiously followed the noise, moving one stiff leg ahead of the other, across the kitchen to the rear entrance. He made a right turn down the long back hallway.

"SHOUP, SHOUP-PAH-KE-E-EW!"

The noise seemed to be coming from the den. The door to the den was closed. It was all the way at the end of the hall.

"SHOUP, SHOUP, SHOUP-PAH-KE-E-EW!"

It seemed forever before Henkin reached the closed door. The noise was louder now. God only knew what was going on behind that closed door!

"SHOUP, SHOUP, SHOUP-PAH-KE-E-EW!"

Should he open the door? Should he go back to the telephone? Should he call for help?

"SHOUP, PAH-KE-E-E-E-EW!"

Henkin opened the door.

Jeff looked up, startled. He was sitting cross-legged on the floor in front of the television, manipulating the joystick of his Atari video-game set. He was playing "Asteroids"—with a vengeance. The volume control of the television was turned up full blast.

"SHOUP, SHOUP-PAH-KE-E-EW!" The game screamed at them both.

Henkin was angry at first.

"*Chalerya!* For this you don't come to Bar Mitzvah lessons?"

Then Henkin saw the scratches and bruises on Jeff's face and the ace bandage wrapped around Jeff's ankle.

"*Gott in himmel! Tayerer kind,* what happened?"

Jeff told Henkin about the locker room. He did not mention the names of Keith Anderson or the other boys in the gang. Nearly in tears, he told what had become of his Maftir booklet.

"Nazi bastards," said Henkin. "Nazi bastards. They're all over the world."

"They're not Nazis, Henkin," Jeff said. "Just tough kids. It's their way of having fun. Even if it's a weird way. They're not *real* Nazis."

"They're Nazis," Henkin insisted. "I know. That's what Nazis are. They must be stopped."

"Huh? What are you talking about?"

"First, the shul. Now, you. Nazis must be stopped."

"Henkin, I'm all right. The school nurse looked at me. She said my bruises are minor. The bandage on my ankle is just for a day or two. It happens. It's part of school."

"The Nazis take over whatever they can, if people let them. They have to be stopped *before* it's too late. It must never happen again."

Henkin left the room to start preparing dinner. Alone in the kitchen, he reached into his pocket and took out a folded handbill he had found lying on the sidewalk between the Lazarus house and the synagogue. He read it through once more—he had read it a dozen times—and made a sour face. Then he placed the handbill down on the kitchen counter, and took the chicken cutlets out of the refrigerator.

Jeff kept on playing "Asteroids." As a concession to Henkin, he lowered the volume. Nevertheless, each time he shot and pulverized an asteroid, Jeff imagined that it was Keith and his gang being pulverized.

On the screen, Jeff's "Asteroids" score registered 564,975. He still had seven spaceships to go. He was lost in concentration. He had no idea of the time.

With one more "pah-ke-e-ew" and a high-pitched "beep, beep, beep," Jeff was awarded yet another spaceship. Robert opened the door to the den.

"Where's Henkin?"

"I don't know," said Jeff, not taking his eyes off the screen. "He was just here. Making dinner, I guess."

"SHOUP, SHOUP, SHOUP, PAH-KE-E-EW!"

"He's nowhere in the house," said Robert. There was concern in his voice.

"He's not in the backyard and no one is answering the telephone at the temple," said Terri as she joined Robert in the doorway.

"He was just here a minute ago," said Jeff as he furiously pumped the red button and moved the joystick. He was annoyed by the interruption.

"What time was that?" asked Robert, starting to get equally annoyed at his younger brother.

"I don't know. Five o'clock, maybe. It was after he came home from Bar Mitzvah class. I didn't go today."

"You what?" started Robert.

"Look at him, Robbie," Terri interjected suddenly. "He looks like he went scuba diving in a food processor."

"*Damn*! I just lost a spaceship with all your talking. He was just here. I just talked to him a minute ago."

"Jeff, you little twit. It's nearly seven o'clock! How

long do you think it takes to add up 500,000 points on that stupid thing?" asked Terri.

"Jeff, turn off the Atari and talk to us. What happened to you today? And what happened to Henkin?"

Jeff reluctantly reached for a pad of paper and the pen that were on the lamp table. He wrote:

JEFF

ASTEROIDS # 9

SCORE (WHEN INTERRUPTED): 566,325

SEVEN SHIPS REMAINING

He put the pen and pad down on the rug, flicked the Atari console switch to the off position, reached over to the television set and turned it off. The screen extinguished itself to a small dot of light in the center, then went out.

He stood, wincing at a sharp pain in his taped ankle. Robert and Terri were still in the doorway. With a little touch of pride, Jeff said, "I got beaten up in school today."

"By *whom*?" asked Terri, squinting one eye.

"Does it matter?" responded Jeff.

"Yes, it matters," Terri nagged. "I'll write a note to your principal for you."

"That's the *last* thing I'd want you to do," said Jeff, his eyes pleading with Robert for understanding. Robert nodded. He understood these things better than Terri.

"Who was it?" asked Robert.

"Oh, Keith Anderson and some of his 'dirt' friends."

"Try to avoid them. If they bother you again, let me know. Okay?"

"Sure," said Jeff. "What bothers me is that they tore my Maftir booklet up and kept calling me 'dirty Jew-boy.' "

Terry threw her arms around Jeff and hugged him and kissed him in several places on his red, sore face. Jeff smarted a bit as her embrace squeezed tender bruises on his arms and back.

"Oh, Jeff, my darling brother. I love you. Can I interview you for an article I'm writing for the school newspaper?"

Robert gave Terri a disapproving look. Terri let Jeff go.

"We still have to find Henkin. God knows where he is. He's an old man," said Robert. "Maybe he tripped and fell somewhere. He's *our* responsibility."

"He may have left a note in the kitchen," said Jeff. "Anyway, I smell dinner. It smells like chicken. And the last I talked to him, he said he was going to make dinner."

The three went into the kitchen. Chicken cutlets were in the frying pan on the electric range. They were done. The burner was shut off. It had been cool for a while. There was no note on the refrigerator door where the magnetic note fasteners were hanging. And there was no note on the small cork board by the wall phone.

"Why were you guys so late coming home tonight?" asked Jeff.

"Mary Beth wanted to watch some guys playing basketball after school. She dragged me with her. It took hours before I could drag her away and come home," said Terri.

Robert looked serious. He was sorry that he had come home late to find Henkin gone without even a message.

"I was with Lauryn after school," Robert said, a little embarrassed. Lauryn was his girlfriend. "We took a drive. I had a very aggravating conversation with Brian Epstein at lunch today."

He didn't tell them about the remark Brian had made about their mother. It still upset him to think about it. Not that he thought she hadn't been saved. Brian's idea of saved was whacky. But the remark had made him aware of how much he—they all—missed their mother. He just had to talk about it with Lauryn. All he said to his siblings was, "We drove around a bit. Then we parked and talked. I guess we lost track of time."

"I'll bet," said Terri, knowingly. She really didn't know.

"Did you get anything out of Brian?" asked Jeff. "Did he have something to with the swastika on the synagogue door?"

"I'm not really sure. One thing: He *was* there last night. But first things first. We've got to find Henkin. I wish Dad were home," said Robert. He was worried.

"What's this?" Terri picked up a scrap of newspaper on the kitchen table by the phone. On the margin of the scrap, in pencil, was a telephone number. It was in Henkin's shaky, European handwriting. "555-8088."

"It looks familiar," said Robert. "I know that number, but I just can't remember whose it is."

"Why don't you just call the number and see who answers?" asked Jeff casually.

"Sometimes, for a twit, you're a genius!" exclaimed Terri.

Robert dialed and listened. He put down the receiver. It was Vito's Belwyn Cab Service.

"Let's assume that Henkin took a cab somewhere," Robert said out loud to his brother and sister. "Where would he go suddenly, and without telling anyone, on a Thursday night?"

Terri perked up. "Maybe the newspaper scrap isn't

just something he tore out at random. Maybe that piece of paper can tell us."

Robert looked at it. "It's an ad for a restaurant, the Bavarian Steak and Brew. Sunrise Highway, Belwyn. Oompapa Band nightly. Free shrimp and salad bar. Heinrich Hoffmann, proprietor. Visa and Master-charge accepted. Henkin wouldn't go there! He's more kosher than God!"

"Don't be so sure." It was Jeff. "I just found this on the counter."

Jeff showed them a handbill announcing a meet-ing of the White America Party in the Rhine Room of the Bavarian Steak and Brew. "The meeting is to-night: Thursday."

"Oh, boy," said Robert. "If Henkin went there he's in a lot of trouble. I've heard of the White America Party. They're a neo-Nazi lunatic group."

"That's trouble," Jeff chimed in. "He was on a 'we've got to stop the Nazis' tirade. He even accused the Nazis of beating me up at school."

"Terri, let's get into the car," Robert ordered. "We've got to get Henkin out of there before he gets himself hurt. Or worse."

"I want to go, too," implored Jeff.

"No. You stay home. By the telephone. If we're not back in an hour, call the Fifth Precinct and tell them about Henkin and the meeting."

"I never get to do anything," Jeff pouted.

"It's important for you to stay here," Robert shouted. "Listen to me for once, okay?"

Robert and Terri were already halfway out the front door.

"Okay," Jeff said. The door slammed and the Buick screeched out of the driveway. Jeff watched it go.

Henkin sat at the bar of the Bavarian Steak and Brew.

The bartender eyed him with amusement, serving the regular customers first. He took a long time coming over to the little old Jewish man wearing a grey-plaid, snap-brim rain hat; two-tone, half-black, half-clear framed bifocal eyeglasses; and an outrageous electric blue, double-knit suit. Standing across the counter from Henkin, the bartender raised his voice for the entertainment of the others in the place. "Name your poison, Pop."

"If you please, sir," said Henkin, "I'll have tea, in a glass."

The bartender shrugged theatrically to the chuckles of the other customers. But he brought Henkin tea in a glass from the kitchen. If Henkin was aware of the small scene he was causing, he did not show it.

Henkin turned slightly on the barstool. He held the hot glass of tea in his hand. Long ago, he had grown used to the heat. He looked out at the room full of people talking over the oompapa of the live band and eating their steak platters.

He thought for a moment that he was in another time and place, listening to the same music, seeing the same people he had seen so long ago.

Caught up in his memory, Henkin did not see the bartender whispering to a large-chested, brawny young man who stood nursing a beer at the end of the bar. Henkin paid no attention as the man got up and walked through the entrance to the Rhine Room behind the main dining room. Nor did Henkin see the young man return side by side with Heinrich Hoffmann, the proprietor.

It was only when he turned back toward the bar that Henkin saw Hoffmann approaching him.

There was no mistake! Henkin knew that face at once! Older, perhaps. Much older. But Henkin would never forget that face. It was a face that haunted his dreams.

Herr Hoffmann stopped in front of Henkin's stool.

"Are you enjoying yourself, sir?" asked Hoffmann. His English was laced with traces of a German accent.

"Good tea," Henkin replied. He knew that his own, Yiddish, accent was also noticeable.

"I must tell you, sir, that we have a ten dollar minimum. Can I serve you dinner at a table?"

"Well, I thought just to have some tea and listen, if you please, to the fine music. For ten dollars, I might have another tea."

"Our guests help pay for the music by having dinner," Hoffmann said. "You must have dinner or I must regrettably ask you to leave."

"And who are you to ask me to leave this restaurant? This is Belwyn, New York in the United States of America!"

"I am Heinrich Hoffmann, proprietor of this fine establishment. I am sorry, but it's our policy."

"Heinrich Hoffmann. Herr Hoffmann, were you ever known by another name?"

Hoffmann was taken aback for a moment. He turned to the brawny young man who had already signalled to the Rhine Room, and was joined by an assortment of rough-looking men in their teens and twenties. They formed a half-circle around Henkin who was still seated on the barstool.

"Aw, let him stay. The old man isn't hurting anybody." It was the voice of a young man, sitting with his date at a table near the bar.

One of the teenage thugs turned to the young man who had spoken. With a stiff straight arm and flat palm, he shoved the young man back in his seat. "Shut up and mind your own business."

The young man, wanting not to be embarrassed in the presence of his date, stood up and swung his fist into the grinning teeth of the arrogant teenager. Two other thugs immediately grabbed the diner and started taking punches at him.

The young man's date screamed. The oompapa

band stopped playing. The other diners in the restaurant looked on. There was a shocked silence all around.

Henkin looked like he had seen it all before.

Terri and Robert arrived and parked the Buick directly in front of the main entrance to the restaurant. As they came up to the door, they could see the drama unfolding within through the glass windows of the doors.

"Robbie, we've got to get Henkin out of there!"

"I know, but we've got to think first. We can't just rush in. There are too many of them. Let me *think*."

The fight was spreading. More of the customers rushed to defend the young man. More thugs came out of the Rhine Room. There were punches and groans. Ceramic Bavarian beer mugs were flying and crashing. Some hit the mirrored wall behind the bar, denting the glass and cracking it in places. Now and then a body hit against one of the small tables, sending table and food and plates tumbling into the laps of the dumbfounded diners. The bartender came out from behind the bar to join in. And several of the young, blonde waitresses, dressed like Bavarian tavern maids, were slugging away, too.

In the midst of the melee, Henkin calmly sipped his glass of tea and studied Herr Hoffmann. The proprietor stood still, wondering how the situation had gone out of control.

Outside the Bavarian Steak and Brew, Robert kept mumbling to himself. "Think. Think." Then, "I've got it! Terri, two years ago I studied the Book of Judges with Rabbi Rosen at the Central Hebrew High!"

"Not now, Robbie. C'mon. We've got to *do* something."

"The story of Gideon."

"This is no time for a Bible lesson!"

"Gideon had only a few men, but he defeated the entire Midianite army!"

"For crying out loud, Robbie."

"They panicked an army of thousands with shofars and torches in jugs!"

"C'mon. Tell me."

"Dad keeps a flasher in the trunk of the car in case the car breaks down on the road. It plugs into the cigarette lighter. Dad's C.B. radio also has a P.A. system built into it!"

"Robbie, you're beginning to make sense. I'm with you."

"Here's the key to the trunk, Terri. Hurry."

Terri took the flasher from the trunk and handed it to Robert, along with the car keys.

Robert placed the flasher on the roof of the Buick and plugged the cord into the cigarette lighter. He turned the key in the starter. The light began to flash.

Next he switched the C.B. over to its public address system and blew into the microphone, hearing the sound rasp out loudly in the night air. He raised the microphone to his lips, and in his deepest, most authoritative voice spoke into it. "This is the police. We have you surrounded."

Inside, the fighting stopped for an instant. The flash of lights lit up the dark doorway. Then there were shouts of "Back door! Back door!"

People practically climbed over one another, stampeding to the narrow back door. Robert and Terri raced into the restaurant. They grabbed Henkin, lifting him from the barstool and pulling him bodily out the front door to the waiting car.

"But I didn't pay for my tea. It's ten dollars," protested Henkin.

"This is the police. We have you surrounded."

"Mail them a check," Robert quipped.

They plopped Henkin into the back seat of the car, barely remembered to take the flasher off the roof, and nearly lost the still open door on Terri's side as Robert swiftly backed out of the parking space. Robert hit the brakes, jerked the shift lever into drive, and left a spray of gravel in his wake. He darted onto Sunrise Highway, putting distance between them and the Bavarian Steak and Brew.

They did not say a word to Henkin the rest of the ride. Henkin was not talking, either. He seemed to be in another world.

Robert turned his key and released the lock on the front door of the Lazarus house on Seaville Avenue. He held the door open for Henkin. The old man shuffled into the vestibule. Robert and Terri followed him into the house.

Robert didn't know what to say.

6
Henkin's Story

"What took you so long?" asked Jeff as the trio entered the living room. "I was just about to call the cops."

Robert and Terri helped Henkin to a seat near the window in the front wall of the living room. They hovered over him protectively.

Jeff could see that Henkin's eyes were glazed over, as if his body were here, but his mind somewhere else.

"It's a long story," said Terri to Jeff. "Let's give Henkin a chance to get himself together again."

Jeff crouched down in front of the old man and looked up at him with love and concern. "Henkin . . .?"

Henkin's full name was Joseph Henkin. Yet nobody had ever called him "Joseph" or "Joe" or even "Mr. Henkin." Everyone called him "Henkin." It was as though "Henkin" was his only name. "Henkin" was his essence. Even his late wife, Tillie, had always called him "Henkin."

"Henkin . . .?"

The old man's eyes fixed on Jeff's upturned, pleading face. He looked next at Terri, then at Robert. He was fully in the present now, in the living room of the house on Seaville Avenue.

"Children," said Henkin suddenly, "sit on the floor in front of me. I have a story to tell you. I have kept it inside for forty years."

Robert and Terri sat beside Jeff on the carpet. All three looked up at the wizened, craggy face; and listened, as in days long past disciples sat at the feet of their masters drinking in their words with thirst.

"The town of Beresteczko, in Volhynia, in the Ukraine—that's where I was born. Jews and *goyim* had shared this town since the 1500s. In my time, before the Second World War, there were about two thousand Jews in all.

"Beresteczko was in a border country, always caught between the Poles and the Cossacks or Ukranians. When one or another would rule over the town, they found ways to cause Jews to suffer. At times, the Jews fought back. Often, they suffered. That was the past. But what is past history, when you have your own?

"King Solomon said, '*Ain kawl hodosh tahas hashomesh*,' 'There's nothing new under the sun,' children. With the Ukranians we suffered. With the Poles we suffered. But we got along. We helped one another. We had Jewish organizations—for widows and orphans, for the sick and the poor. And we had a *Tarbut* school in town. The Zionist teachers and group leaders taught Hebrew and Jewish customs in the school. They formed *hachsharot*, small working groups, to teach trades and farming to the Jews who wanted to go to Palestine to build a Jewish homeland. Many of my friends studied at the *Tarbut* school, worked in the *hachsharot*, and went to Palestine in the 1930s. This was in the days before there was a State of Israel.

"My family was more religious than most. I was not allowed to study in the Polish school in town; and, for my parents, *aleichem hasholom*, even the *Tarbut* school was not *frum*, not religious enough. I was sent to a *yeshivah*, a Torah academy. I was a good student. I had a knack for languages. With a little help, I taught myself Polish, Ukranian, and German. This was, of course, in addition to Yiddish, which we all spoke, and *lashon hakodesh,* the Holy Tongue.

"Even so, my choices were few. I did not want to become a rabbi. Being a rabbi in Europe was not like being a rabbi here in America. Few Jews were allowed to go to the university. So, I had to learn a trade. My father was disappointed. He wanted me to be a scholar, a *rav.*

"My father had a tailor shop. He was not like these tailors today who know only to change a sleeve or shorten a leg of your trousers. He was a fine European tailor who made suits for gentlemen.

"At first, he did not want to teach me tailoring. He said it was a waste of my gift for learning. But, in the end, he taught me all he knew—he taught me to be a fine European tailor. All the time he hoped that I would not be good at tailoring, that I would go back to the *yeshivah* to study Talmud. How could he know that being a tailor would save my life?

"When I was twenty, I married Hannah. She was the town beauty, daughter of a fine family. She was just eighteen, and already a leader of one of the Zionist youth groups."

The three young people looked puzzled.

"That's right," Henkin went on, "Tillie, rest her soul, was not my first wife. That is something about Henkin that no one else in Belwyn knows.

"Hannah and I were both young; those were good years for us both. She wanted to move to Palestine. I kept promising to move, then putting it off. Beresteczko was what I knew. If we had left for Palestine before the Russians came, my whole life would have changed. But who knew?

"Even before the Russians and Hitler, life was changing all around us. In a way, I started out like the old Jew—a thin, pale *yeshivah bohur,* all my strength in my head and very little in my muscles. But Hannah was the new kind of Jew. These were the Zionists who came out of the *Tarbut* school and worked in the *hachsharot* where they did planting and plowing, worked in sawmills, and learned heavy construction jobs. When the Ukranian teenagers ran in tough gangs—stealing, beating, and torturing the weak and old Jews—the Zionists stood up to them and fought back. They were not afraid."

Henkin cleared his throat. He sat quietly for a moment, staring out through the window. Then he began again, "From 1936 on, we heard of Hitler and read about what was happening in Germany. It seemed far away. We heard the Jews were suffering. We thought it was the old kind of suffering—the pain of exile, of having no homeland. What was so new about anti-Semitism, anyway? But in 1939, Hitler conquered Poland from the West; and the Russian army seized parts of Poland, including Beresteczko, from the East.

"The Russians closed the *Tarbut* school. They sent many of the Jewish leaders away. They closed down the Jewish organizations. Many of the Zionist leaders fled to avoid arrest. The Russians closed down all the small shops and made the tradespeople form 'cooperatives.' There was a carpenters' cooperative, a shoemakers' cooperative, and my father and I became part of the tailors' cooperative. The Russians were teaching us communism.

"The Russians ruled over Beresteczko nearly three years. In the first year, my mother died of cancer. She was only in her fifties; and we thought it a great tragedy that she died so young. My children, Mordecai and Dovid—then only five and three—could hardly understand the weeping and mourning that took place at the funeral and in the seven days of *shiva*. We thought God was cruel to take her from us so soon; how could we know the suffering that God had spared her?

"I'll never forget, it was a Sunday—June 22, 1942—when the Germans marched into town. The Ukranians called them liberators; they came out of church to throw flowers on the marching Nazi soldiers. The Ukranians and the Germans had much in common: both hated the Russians and both hated the Jews.

"My father at first thought nothing would really change. We tailors stayed working at the cooperative. We were making custom uniforms for the German officers. That's how I met one young Nazi officer, Lieutenant Kurt Hammerstein.

"He posed like a Nordic god in front of the mirror in our fitting room. I learned his every measurement, down to the last centimeter. I tell you he was impressive. As I crouched by his feet to mark material with my tailor's chalk, I stole quick glances up at this magnificent strong man. He never looked down. He paid no attention to me at all. I only knew he was pleased by the way he looked proudly at himself in the mirror as his uniform took shape.

"In late July, the uniform was finished—all but some final stitches and trim. It was a handsome uniform; and I had done a good job. The Germans had been in town a month, and all seemed normal. I began to think that the stories and rumors we heard about Jewish suffering at German hands were all false.

"Suddenly, one summer's day near the end of July, the Germans and some of the Ukranian gangsters rounded up three hundred Jewish men. My father was one of them. There was no rhyme or reason—some were old, some young. They took them to the outskirts of town, forced them to dig a big pit, then lined them up and shot them. They threw the Jewish bodies into the pit and buried them there.

"By sundown, we all heard what had happened. I even learned that my 'customer,' the handsome young officer, was the one who led the platoon that did the shooting. The next day, he came to pick up his finished uniform. He stood before the mirror, trying it on, pleased with how it fit. He spoke to me for the first time. He told me I did nice work. Do you believe it? The day before, he murdered my father; that day, he said I did nice work!

"This time, there was no funeral, no seven days of mourning. The Germans made us work from dawn to late at night, every day of the week. No more *Shabbos*. They put the Jews to work making uniforms for the German soldiers. Hannah worked at making woolen socks. Her mother watched over our two boys.

"Pretty soon, they set aside a small part of Beresteczko and called it the Jewish "ghetto." Every Jew had to live in this small space. We had to share our homes. People died from the work. We had to share our food. Many died of hunger; even more died of diseases. There was no medicine.

The Germans treated me better than most. Because I could speak German, they made me supervisor of the tailoring factory. They allowed me to go back and forth between the ghetto and the non-Jewish part of town. I smuggled food into the ghetto from outside. They seemed to trust me. They never searched me, though more than once I was afraid they would.

"In the fall of 1942, the German soldiers went from house to house, herding all the Jews of Beresteczko into the main street of the ghetto. There were only about seven hundred of us left, then. I happened to be on a buying trip, outside the ghetto, meeting with a *goy* to buy woolen material for uniform making. Outside the window of the room where we met, there was a park. A German oompapa band was playing, and

German officers and their lady friends were having a picnic.

"Very few Jews—a handful—escaped the German roundup that day. One was a man who worked with me in the uniform shop. At the last moment, he darted into a narrow basement green cellar. Through a crack in the wooden door, he saw what happened in the main street. Later, he told me.

"Lieutenant Hammerstein, wearing the uniform I made for him, tortured many Jews—just for fun, to show off his cruelty to his men. One of these was my Hannah. She stood holding our two darling sons, protecting them. As Hammerstein came near her with his pistol drawn, she shielded their eyes.

"In a loud voice—so his men could hear—Hammerstein told Hannah that the Germans were just following orders. But, he was kind, he said. It was a shame to see two such nice young boys die. Perhaps, he could arrange to save one of them. If Hannah would choose which one should live, Hammerstein said, he would shoot the other cleanly through the head. It would save at least one boy the walk through the woods, he announced.

"Can you imagine such a choice? My Hannah screamed. She lunged at Hammerstein, tearing an epaulet from the shoulder of his uniform before one of the soldiers caught and held her. This seemed to outrage Hammerstein. He turned coldly and murdered my two sons. Two pistol shots, right before Hannah's eyes.

"This was not enough for him. He wanted to show his men that he was an Aryan of steel. He turned again on his polished black boots, ordered the soldier to release my Hannah; and as she ran toward him in hysteria, he leveled his pistol coolly and fired off a third shot. Hannah fell dead.

"Hammerstein killed a few more children and tortured a few of the older Jews until, at last, the whole group was led off into the woods outside town. Of those who marched off that day, none lived."

"I saw the Jews being marched out as I was walking back toward the ghetto. I hid until dark, then I could wait no longer. I wanted to get back to see if there would be any news—any news at all—of Hannah and the children having escaped. Even then, I knew in my heart it was a false hope.

"Under cover of darkness, I slipped back into the ghetto. In truth, I could not think of another place to go. All I knew was Beresteczko.

"In a dark alley I felt a hand grip my shoulder. I thought my end had come. But it was Lensky, the young tailor who told me what happened to my Hannah and my sons. He said he had a plan to escape. He told me to go with him. As far as he knew, we were the only survivors left. I did not know what else to do. I followed him through the streets and alleys. We dashed for the woods. How we made it past the Germans and Ukranians, I will never know.

"We hid in the cold river water, near the pilings of the sawmill. German patrols came by during the night, but none saw us. All night we waited. My body lost all feeling from the cold, dark water. My heart had no feeling left since I heard the story of Hannah, Mordecai and Dovidl.

"Lensky told me that an old Polish friend of his was part of a partisan group who attacked the Germans from the dense woods around Beresteczko. Just before dawn, we made our way deep into the woods. We did not find the partisans, they found us. A voice from behind suddenly spoke to us in Polish, and before we knew it the partisans were all around us.

"Lensky and I became partisans, then. Your Henkin learned how to make and set explosive charges. More than once, our partisan group blew up

German truck convoys as they passed the highways beside the woods. I survived the rest of 1943 and part of 1944 in the woods, among the Poles. Lensky, the only other Jew, who was younger and stronger than I, was killed in a mission against a German patrol.

"In the spring of 1944, the Russian army recaptured Beresteczko, driving the Germans out. By that time, I was far away. Our group had moved southwest to the area around Tarnapol. We met there a group of Jewish partisans, and I left behind the Poles and joined the Jews. I spent the rest of the war with these partisans, still helping to make and set explosives.

"After the war, I lived in the woods for a few more months. There was no family left for me to return to in Beresteczko. I didn't want to live under the Russians and their communism. Slowly, the group split up. Three of us walked westward across Europe to an American zone. We were already experts at passing borders and getting by all kinds of authorities. Strangely, we ended up in Augsburg, in Germany. That was where the Americans were. We reached them in 1946 and they put us in a Displaced Persons Camp.

"In that camp, I met Tillie. She had lost all her family, as I had lost mine. She had never been married, for the Nazis came and interrupted that part of her life. She had survived a concentration camp and been liberated by the Americans. Because of what the Nazi doctors had done to her, she knew she could never have children. But we fell in love. She was then in her early thirties, and I was thirty-seven.

"We were married in the camp by an Orthodox American rabbi who had come with the American army. Tillie had a cousin in New York, an American citizen, who sponsored us and brought us to America. We came in 1947. I found work as a tailor.

"This is where I'll end my story," said Henkin. He sighed and rested, as though he had just put down a very heavy burden.

"It's so hard to believe," said Jeff. "And it happened to someone we know!"

"Henkin," said Terri, "please let me write your story down. People should know. We can't let that kind of world ever happen again."

"Yes, Terri," responded Henkin. "You can write it down. You'll do it well, too, I know. You see why a swastika on a *shul* and Jeff being beaten as a Jew is no light thing to me? That's how it started in Beresteczko. That's how it always starts."

"But, Henkin," interjected Robert, "this is America. It's different. You won't see the people that made Jews suffer in Europe."

"I saw one tonight," said Henkin.

"What?" the three listeners sputtered in unison.

"Herr Heinrich Hoffmann, proprietor of the Bavarian Steak and Brew, is none other than Lieutenant Kurt Hammerstein!" .

"You mean he's *like* Hammerstein," said Robert.

"No. He *is* Kurt Hammerstein. He's changed his name. He's older. But I recognized him clearly. I'll never forget that butcher so long as I live."

Robert sat, lost in thought. The other two were still trying to absorb what Henkin was telling them. Finally, Robert said, "Henkin, there's not much we can do about it tonight. It's late. Get to bed. You've been through a lot this evening. Sleep on it. Tomorrow morning, we can all think about this with clearer heads."

Jeff helped Henkin to get up, and helped him to walk toward his bedroom.

As Jeff and Henkin left the living room arm in arm—the one limping on his injured ankle and the other shuffling heavily in his usual way—they seemed to symbolize the bridge of generations, now tightly bound in empathy. Robert turned to Terri and said, "I wish Dad were home."

7
At the Belwyn Jewish Center

Friday morning.

Rabbi Rosen and Henkin sat side by side in the last pew of the sanctuary, copies of the heavy Hertz *Pentateuch* open on their laps.

Russel Himmelfarb was at the cantor's lectern on the *bimah* platform, chanting his *haftorah*. It was ten o'clock in the morning. In approximately twenty-four-and-a-half hours, Russel would be chanting his *haftorah* "for real" at his Bar Mitzvah ceremony. He had been taking weekly lessons with Henkin for nearly a year. In between lessons, Russel used a cassette tape recording to learn his *haftorah* and the blessings line-by-line at home. By now, the day before the Bar Mitzvah, every member of the Himmelfarb family knew Russel's portion of the Prophets by heart, including the non-Jewish cleaning lady. In fact, most of them could do a better job than Russel. For Russel had no ear for music, a terrible voice, and knew no more than seventeen of the twenty-two letters of the Hebrew alphabet.

The "last rehearsal," on Friday morning before the Saturday of a Bar Mitzvah was an unwritten tradition at the Belwyn Jewish Center. It meant, of course, taking that day off from public school. But everyone concerned understood the stakes. Aside from the last chance to "walk through" the ceremony, including all the Hebrew chanting and English speeches, it was the day on which the women of the family had appointments at the beauty parlor and the men—including the Bar Mitzvah boy—had their hair cut. The rehearsal was scheduled for the morning so as not to conflict with these appointments.

Russel chanted on, doing pretty well. *"Va-yomer Shmuel et kawl Yisrael . . ."*

"El *kawl Yisrael!"* shouted Rabbi Rosen from the back pew. The rabbi turned his head to Henkin.

Henkin shrugged his shoulders. "He's been making that mistake for at least nine months. I've even written 'E-L' in English letters over that word in his *Maftir* booklet. He has lots of words written in English letters in his *Maftir* booklet." Henkin looked apologetic. Tomorrow was Shabbat *Korah*. The congregation would read the story of Korah and his opposition to Moses. Henkin thought, Maybe God will be merciful and the ground will swallow us all up.

Rabbi Rosen called out to Russel again, "El *kawl Yisrael. Va-yomer Shmuel* el *kawl Yisrael . . .* Start that verse over again."

Russel did as instructed. He seemed to be in a daze. The interruption broke his limited sense of melody and rhythm. It took him a moment to find his place.

Russel chanted, *"Va-yomer Shmuel el kawl Yisrael, hinei shama'ti . . ."*

"Good," said Rabbi Rosen. "Now do it just one more time, to make sure.

Russel hesitated, then chanted, *"Va-yomer Shmuel et kawl Yisrael . . ."*

Rabbi Rosen winced and said "Keep going."

Russel chanted on, oblivious.

Henkin smiled. "The spoiling of the generations, *kilkul ha-doros,"* he whispered to the rabbi. Henkin's theory was that each generation got progressively worse Jewishly so that finally the Messiah would *have* to come. To Henkin, Russel was doing his best to usher in the Days of the Messiah.

Russel droned on.

"At least his mistakes are well memorized," said Rabbi Rosen to Henkin. The rabbi knew that the overwhelming majority of Hebrew school students did well in their Bar Mitzvah and Bat Mitzvah preparations. Almost all of them went on to post-Bar/Bat Mitzvah classes, or to the more intensive Central Hebrew High School. There were even a few Jewish Day School students in his congregation. He wasn't worried.

He whispered to Henkin, "Russel's basically a good kid. He'll be a *shul* joiner when he grows up. He'll be a loyal rank-and-file Jew, you'll see."

"He doesn't keep kosher or *Shabbos*. He can't even read Hebrew," said Henkin under his breath. "What kind of Jew can he be?"

"A synagogue president," said the rabbi with a wink of his eye.

At that moment, B. B. Braverman entered the sanctuary, a visibly agitated Vivian Himmelfarb— Russel's mother—right behind him.

B. B. bent over the back pew and whispered into Rabbi Rosen's ear, "Rabbi, can we see you out in the hall a minute? There's something that has to be settled. I even took off from the store for this."

Russel chanted on. He did not even notice the rabbi leaving the sanctuary with his mother and the President of Belwyn Jewish Center.

In the hallway, outside the closed doors of the sanctuary, Vivian Himmelfarb spoke first. "Rabbi, how could you do this to us? After all the hours my husband and I spent working at the Temple bazaar!"

"Pardon?" said Rabbi Rosen, calmly. He guessed at what was coming.

"How could you tell them to leave that *mess* up on

the door on the weekend of our Bar Mitzvah? A *swastika!* 'Kill the Jews!' It's just terrible. What will we tell the cousins from California? They belong to a beautiful temple out there. They've always been a little snobbish about the Long Island part of the family. What will they say? That we live in a slum?"

"Well," began Rabbi Rosen, but there was no stopping Mrs. Himmelfarb at this point.

"We've a good mind to resign from the congregation after the Bar Mitzvah."

B. B. Braverman blanched. These words were the last thing he liked hearing. "Calm down, Vivian. Can I call you Vivian? I'm sure we can work it out."

Vivian Himmelfarb ignored him. She looked straight at the young rabbi, a sense of betrayal on her face and in her voice as she went on.

"We were so careful in planning this function. We tipped Johnny extra to clean the trash from the roots of the hedges on the temple lawn. We made sure that he cleaned the mens' and ladies' rooms behind the ballroom so they wouldn't be the disgrace they were at Gladys Untermeyer's function for Wendy. Remember? What do we pay dues for? And, all those years of Hebrew school carpooling? For spray-painted doors at *my* Bar Mitzvah? Now, because of *you,* Rabbi, we'll never be able to set foot in California!"

"Now, Vivian," said B. B. "It's still early enough in the day to sand the doors and have them repainted. Right, Rabbi? *Shabbos* comes late this time of year, right? We could have everything done in time, couldn't we?"

"Mrs. Himmelfarb," said Rabbi Rosen, "did you see today's *Newsday* yet?"

"Who has time to read newspapers? I had to pick up my gown at the dressmaker and I still have a million things to do for the Bar Mitzvah. Rabbi, you don't even know what a Bar Mitzvah is!"

"Well, there's an article in today's paper about the

spray-painting of our synagogue, with a photograph. You can cut it out for the California cousins to see. This kind of anti-Semitic vandalism has become countrywide. It happens in California, too. Tell your guests that our synagogue has left the markings up as part of our way of combatting this epidemic. When the culprits are caught, whether they're kids or not, we'll have the *culprits* sand the doors and repaint them. I'll be speaking about the swastika in my sermon tomorrow. All your guests will understand what we are doing here at the Belwyn Jewish Center."

"What about Russel and his friends? A Bar Mitzvah is such a big event in his life. Did it have to be *this* weekend, of all weekends?"

"We didn't plan it," said the rabbi, consoling her. "But Bar Mitzvah means coming into adult Jewish life. For Russel, it will add even more meaning to this event. We Jews cannot hide our heads and pretend that things like this never happen. Russel will see that we respond through legal means to nip anti-Semitism in the bud, before it grows really menacing. Leaving the swastika up will enhance the meaning of Russel's Bar Mitzvah ceremony—for Russel, and for everyone present."

"Maybe you're right; maybe you're not, Rabbi," said Vivian. "But you had better be sure to mention in your sermon that the swastika *just* happened, and that the temple doesn't *always* look like that!"

"Of course."

"Well, then. Leave it up, I guess. By the way, thank you for helping Russel with his speeches. We couldn't think of a thing for him to write."

"My pleasure. He's a good kid. You'll all be proud of him tomorrow."

"We'll see you later tonight at services. We sit in the front pew, right?"

"That's right."

"We've never sat in the front row before."

"No one ever does, until a *simhah*. Front rows everywhere seem to be automatically reserved for special occasions."

"See you later, Rabbi. I've really got a million things to do."

"*Shabbat shalom,*" the rabbi said. B. B. muttered a goodbye.

Vivian Himmelfarb turned to go down the steps from the sanctuary floor to the first floor. She was joined by Russel who had just finished his rehearsal with Henkin alone.

Henkin called out a quick, "*Mazal tov,*" to Mrs. Himmelfarb. He was thinking that she'd need it.

With the Himmelfarbs gone, B. B. gave a sigh of relief. He smiled at Rabbi Rosen and jokingly said, "Remember, Rabbi, I'm behind you ninety-nine percent." Then he walked down the steps after the Himmelfarbs.

Rabbi Rosen looked at Henkin. "Yesterday, he was behind me one hundred percent."

Henkin did not tell Rabbi Rosen about Thursday night. Henkin wanted to be absolutely certain about Heinrich Hoffmann, first.

Rabbi Rosen congratulated Henkin on the job he had done preparing Russel. "Not an easy case," he added.

The rabbi started thinking about his sermon for Saturday morning. He stepped out the side door of the synagogue for some air and sun to help his thinking along. Looking over toward the parking lot, he noticed that the sedan which was dented last Wednesday night, the night of the spray painting, by the fleeing yellow car, was still parked in the same spot. No one had moved it, so it seemed, since Wednesday night.

Out of curiosity, Rabbi Rosen went over and jotted down the sedan's license number in the pocket calendar book he carried with him every day, except *Shabbat*.

Back in his study, inside the *shul*, Rabbi Rosen telephoned the Fifth Precinct and asked for Officer Oates.

"You're in luck, Rabbi," the clerk said. "He's right here. Another minute and he would have left for patrol. I'll put him on."

"Yo, Rabbi. This is Oates."

"How's the spray-painting of the Belwyn Jewish Center going? Any leads in the case?"

"I'm not really permitted to give you information at this time, Rabbi. I can say that we're doing our best to try to apprehend the perpetrator. I'm following up on the eyewitness report of the yellow vehicle. If that proves operational, I'll let you know."

"Well, thank you, I guess, Officer Oates. By the way, that sedan the lady said was struck by the yellow car last Wednesday night is still in our parking lot. Here's the license plate number. Can you trace it so that I can inform the owner about the accident and ask him to move his car? We have a Bar Mitzvah this weekend, so we'll need all the spaces in the parking lot."

"For you, Rabbi, I'll run it through the computer. It will only take a second."

Rabbi Rosen read the number to the policeman. The rabbi's call was put on hold. A few minutes later, Officer Oates was back on the line.

"According to the computer, Rabbi, the car is registered in the name of a Heinrich Hoffmann, 207 Sage Street, about two miles away from your synagogue."

"Thanks a lot, Officer. I'll tell him about the fender-bender. I'll bet he'll be glad to hear from me."

8
T.G.I.F. at School

Terri Lazarus fidgeted in her tablet-arm chair in Mr. Rosetti's biology class. She was chewing at her purple polished thumbnail and glancing nervously from time to time at Mary Beth. Christine Mobley and her girlfriends were sitting together along the back row, writing and passing gossipy notes to one another in between drawing aimless fashion doodles on the lined paper of their loose leaf notebooks.

Mr. Rosetti had already marked yesterday's exams—in record time for him—and was about to hand the papers back to the class.

Terri stared at the stack of papers in Mr. Rosetti's hands. She was playing out "worst-case scenarios" in her mind. What would she say at home about her low grade? How could she study harder for the next exam?

"I felt it was a fair exam," began Mr. Rosetti. "The grades can be plotted on a bell-shaped curve, ranging from forty to a hundred. There was only one perfect paper, though."

When Mr. Rosetti said, "only one perfect paper," all the students looked toward Terri. Christine said it out loud for the class. "And Terri Lazarus is the hundred." There was a cutting edge to her tone.

Terri turned to the back row. She had an "oh, no, not me, not this time" look on her face.

The papers were handed out.

Mary Beth was ecstatic. She had received a ninety. She beamed at Terri.

Christine and her three friends all scored forty. They always sat together, especially during exams.

Terri had gotten the hundred.

"Well, class," said Mr. Rosetti, "let's go over the exam and review the edifying details about the life and loves of Rana *pipiens*. Terri, will you please enlighten your fellow classmates with the answer to the first question?"

Terri gave the correct answer . . . very quietly.

Jeff walked to his next-period class at the junior high. It was Social Studies. Today they would study American ethnic heritages, the great immigrations to America from Europe beginning in the 1880s and going on to the 1920s. Jeff was eager to get to this class because today they would see a filmstrip on the Jews of the Lower East Side of New York. Jeff had already seen this same filmstrip in Hebrew school at the B.J.C., but was strangely happy that it would also be shown in public school.

Jeff was among the "Jewish authorities" in the junior high. His home life and his interest in Hebrew school and synagogue made him a relative "expert" when compared to the few other Jewish kids in his class. At times, this pleased Jeff. Sometimes, it made him feel uneasy.

In any case, today, among his schoolbooks Jeff was carrying a book from his father's collection called *How We Lived*. It had lots of photographs of Jews in New York in this period. He was going to share it with the class. A "Jewish spokesman," he thought, had special responsibilities. It was a rough life, being a living symbol.

His ankle still smarted from yesterday, but what hurt him more was a sense of humiliation for being caught off guard and surrounded by Keith Anderson and his gang. True, they were bigger than he, and he had been forced to face them alone. True, he had kicked Keith and hurt him. But, nevertheless, he wondered if he had fought enough.

An Israeli wouldn't just take it, thought Jeff. Moreover, he now knew that even frail, scholarly Henkin was a fighter. Robbie had said to avoid Keith Anderson, to stay out of trouble. Maybe Robbie was right. But how could he avoid Keith Anderson? Especially now. Keith would be looking for him. It could go on and on. Esau picks on Jacob. Jacob finally kicks Esau where it hurts. Esau torments Jacob even more, claiming to be the injured party. Why, the only way to avoid Keith Anderson would be to leave for another planet! Even the Jews in his picture book had come to America to avoid the Keith Andersons of the world.

"Jeff, do you have an extra pen or pencil? I lost my pen," said Lewis Lewison, as the two of them approached the door of the Social Studies classroom.

Jeff fumbled about his books and pockets. Not only did Jeff not find an extra pen, he discovered that he no longer had the pen *he* was writing with in the last period. Kids his age were constantly losing pens. No problem. Robbie had long ago taught him to keep extra pens in his locker. He had a whole unopened pack on the top shelf there.

"Listen, Lewis," said Jeff, "You take my books to class. I'll run to get two pens. There's still a little time before class starts."

"Okay. Thanks, Jeff. By the way, where were you at Bar Mitzvah lessons yesterday? I thought you never cut lessons. You've got Henkin at home to answer to."

"I was unavoidably detained. Look, I'd better hurry or else be late for class."

"All right, see you in a couple of minutes."

Jeff stepped briskly downstairs to the locker room.

"In a hurry, Little Jeffrey?"

Keith Anderson was leaning against Jeff's locker. He had a fat lip, like someone had punched him in the mouth. "Good," thought Jeff, "violence begets violence. Serves him right." Jeff looked around. At least this time Keith was alone.

"I won't forget yesterday, Little Jeffrey."

"Look, Keith. I don't want any trouble. Let's forget it, okay?"

"You've already got trouble, Little Jeffrey. I'll be watching you from now on."

"C'mon, Keith, let's drop it. I'm sorry I kicked you. I hope you're feeling all right."

"Well, I'm not all right; and you're a marked man, Little Jeffrey. It may not be today. Maybe not tomorrow. But my friends and I won't forget."

"Keith, I've got to get something from my locker and get to class. Please let me open the door."

Surprisingly, Keith stepped aside.

Jeff turned the combination on his lock and hooked the open ring of the lock through the hole of the locker door now swung ajar. He stood on the floor of the locker to reach the box of pens on the top shelf. Keith said, "If you know what's good for you, you won't tell anyone about yesterday."

Still reaching up, Jeff said, "Of course, I won't."

"And this will help you remember." Keith shoved Jeff into the locker and slammed the door, locking it with Jeff's lock.

No one else was in the locker room.

Keith casually walked away, smiling and combing his hair with a pocket comb. His denim jacket with its cut-off sleeves had a swastika patch on its back, along with patches carrying the name of rock bands like Kiss and the Rolling Stones.

In the cramped darkness of the locker, Jeff turned himself around so that he faced the inside of the door.

He pounded with his fists on the metal, shouting for help.

But the period had already begun. There were no students in the locker room. All the teachers were teaching. There was no one to answer his cries for help. The entire world of the Belwyn Junior High School went about its daily routine. Jeff thought, when a tree falls in the forest and no one is around to hear it, it really doesn't make a sound.

Inside the locker, he stopped pounding and shouting. He had never felt so alone before. Even when his mother died, he still had his family. He wished his father were home. Why did he have to go away so much?

It was impossible to straighten up in the locker. Jeff had to hunch his head and shoulders over, so that as the minutes slowly went by, his body started to ache. He felt all yesterday's bruises, and a new one or two that he just got when he was shoved into this little metal prison.

"Henkin wasn't so wrong about life," thought Jeff. "Here I am, just like Henkin, alone, bent over. I can't even move my body.

"Henkin always talks about Jews being alone. We always smile at him. Right now, I don't feel like smiling. No one knows or cares that I'm trapped in here.

"Henkin is right. I can't just let this happen to me all the time. Henkin fought back. So will I. But, how? Robbie says to avoid trouble. But, I can't. I've already got trouble.

"Will they ever find me in here? How long can a person live without food or water? They've got to come to their lockers sometime today. The kids will get me out. What if they don't want to? Robbie will come looking for me. Would he think to come to my locker?"

Then Jeff thought about God. "Does God really know everything that happens? Is God watching me now? Why did my mother have to die? Am I going to die in this locker?"

Jeff did not have much room. He tried reaching into his pants pocket to get to his *kipah*. He could just manage it. He put the *kipah* up on his head. He tried to pray.

Jeff knew the *Alenu* prayer by heart. It was the only one he could think of just then. Inside the locker, he softly chanted the *Alenu,* all the way through to the word *"v'ne'emar."* He didn't understand all the Hebrew, but something told him it was appropriate.

Upstairs, in the Social Studies classroom, Mr. Tucker took roll. When he came to Jeff's name and got no answer, he looked up from his roll book.

"Where's Jeff Lazarus? He never cuts. I know he was especially looking forward to today's class."

"I was with him before class," said Lewis. "I even have his books here. He was going to the lockers to get some pens. He'll be here in a minute."

Mr. Tucker finished taking roll. Jeff still had not arrived.

"Well, maybe Jeff was delayed by some teacher's errand," said Mr. Tucker. "We'll start the filmstrip."

Mr. Tucker turned out the lights and started the projector and the cassette tape recorder. By the time the still photographs showed scenes of a fire and the sound track spoke of a Triangle Shirtwaist Company, Mr. Tucker caught Lewis' eye and motioned him to come over.

"Lewis," said Mr. Tucker. "Here's a hall pass. Go down to the locker room and look for Jeff."

Inside the locker, Jeff had finished the prayer. There was silence all around him. "Jonah in the belly of the fish," thought Jeff. "My punishment for thinking I could avoid Keith."

"Dear God," Jeff said, "if You get me out of this, I promise to be a fighter like Henkin. No more swasti-

77

kas. No more bullying. I'll be a champion of Your people. Please, just send me a sign."

Silence.

Jeff was on the verge of sobbing.

"Jeff? Jeff, are you here?" It was Lewis Lewison. Jeff recognized his voice.

Jeff started banging on the inside of the locker door again. "In here, Lewis. In here!"

Lewis bent close to the outside of Jeff's locker. "What are you doing in there?"

"Never mind. Just get me out."

"I can't. It's locked."

"I *know* it's locked. I'll give you the combination. Turn it left twice to 18, then right to 24, then back to 10."

"What?"

"18-24-10!"

Lewis fumbled with the dial. "Jeff, it won't open."

Jeff had a sickening thought that Keith might have switched locks. Then he thought of Lewis and Lewis' usual clumsiness.

"Try it again, Lewis. I'll tell you slowly."

Finally, the lock came open. Lewis opened the door and Jeff climbed out of the locker.

"How could anybody get locked in his own locker?" asked Lewis, wide-eyed.

"If Keith Anderson shoved you in and locked it," answered Jeff.

"Keith Anderson! Boy, have you got trouble. What are you going to do?"

"I'm not sure yet. Why'd you come looking for me?"

"Mr. Tucker sent me. Hey, we'd better get back to class."

Jeff closed the locker door and fixed the lock. The two boys went upstairs.

The filmstrip was over and the lights were back on in the classroom.

"Jeff, what happened? You were so psyched up for this class," Mr. Tucker said as Jeff and Lewis entered the room.

"I had a stomach ache," Jeff stammered.

Mr. Tucker looked dubious, but he let it pass. Jeff was a good student, with a good record for conduct.

"Okay, take your seats."

Jeff sat in the empty desk beside Lewis. His books were already there. Mr. Tucker wrote the homework assignment on the chalkboard. Jeff looked at Lewis. He had forgotten the pens!

He leaned over to Sherry Silver and asked her if he could borrow a couple of pens for himself and Lewis.

"You boys are never prepared," Sherry said.

It was the end of the school day. Robert sat on the lawn by the student parking lot, waiting for Lauryn. When he saw her coming out of the exit door, he got up and walked over to her.

"Lauryn," he said, "how about going with me to Friday services tonight? I want to see how the congregation reacts to the swastika. And I want to hear what the rabbi is going to say about it."

Lauryn looked down. She did not answer right away.

When she finally looked up, she said, "I can't, Robbie. I've got another date for tonight."

"You mean, you've got to be home with family?"

"No, Robbie, I mean a date."

"Oh," Robert sensed something very wrong. "We're still on for Saturday night, aren't we?"

A long pause.

"Robbie, I've been thinking about this for a while. I find it hard to say, since I like you and all—as a *person*—but my mother thinks we've been seeing too much of each other. We should date other people."

"But, why?" Robert was trying hard to sound adult and strong, and not to let his voice crack.

"It's nothing bad about you, Robbie. I respect you a lot. Everyone does. But everything with you is the synagogue and religion, and very heavy. I'm really not religious."

"Well, I don't mind, really, Lauryn," said Robbie, noticing that his voice was beginning to break up a little.

"Well, you should. We just aren't right for one another. I want to date other people. I want to cool our relationship a while."

Lauryn looked over at him. "We can still be friends, can't we?"

Robert thought, Why do they always say that? He said, "Sure." But he knew he didn't want to be "just" Lauryn's friend. He wanted to be her boyfriend.

"Lauryn, can I drive you home? I still have the car till my Dad gets back."

"No, Robbie. I've got a ride." She looked out to the parking lot brightly and waved. Then she turned to Robbie and said, "See you Monday, in school." She ran off to Stuart Yablon and sat very close to him in his new Toyota. Robert watched as they drove off together.

Robert started walking toward the space where he had left the Lazarus family Buick.

A Nassau County Police Department squad car was parked between the Buick and a yellow Camaro. Robbie could see the bumper stickers.

Officer Oates was speaking with a visibly upset Brian Epstein. Then the policeman opened the back door of the squad car and Brian got in. Officer Oates walked around to the driver's side, sat on his front seat, radioed ahead, and drove off.

Robert could see Brian turn around on the back seat and stare at him from the back window. There was a scared, pleading look on his face.

"Good," said Robert. "They're going to nail that jerk, Brian Epstein. I've got my own problems."

Almost immediately after he said it, Robert was angry with himself. "Not good. I don't think Brian had anything to do with the swastika."

9
Preparing for Shabbat

Erev Shabbat.

Rabbi Rosen finished writing his sermon by mid-Friday afternoon. He stretched the fingers of his right hand a bit to relieve a touch of writer's cramp.

Next item: to call this Heinrich Hoffmann and let him know his car had been on the Belwyn Jewish Center parking lot at an unfortunate moment.

For perhaps the tenth time that day, Rabbi Rosen reached for the Nassau County telephone book. The phone book, he thought, the twentieth century rabbi's reference.

He found the listing and played the number on the push button dial. An elderly woman's voice answered.

"Hello?"

"Mr. Hoffmann, please," the rabbi said.

"He's not in."

Click.

Rabbi Rosen sat for a few seconds looking at the silent receiver in his hand. She had hung up! But Hoffmann really should know about his car. The rabbi dialed again.

"Hello?"

"Ma'am, I must reach Mr. Hoffmann."

"Who *is* this?"

"Rabbi Rosen of . . ."

"Did you say *rabbi*?"

"Yes, of the Belwyn Jewish . . ."

Click.

She did it again. Rabbi Rosen dialed again. The telephone rang and rang and rang.

Rabbi Rosen began speculating. "Maybe the woman is senile. I'll drive over to the Hoffmann house. It's close by. Then I'll make ready for Shabbat."

Rabbi Rosen drove his '66 black Chevy Nova to the Belwyn address given him by Officer Oates. He parked at the curbside in front of a small, tidy-looking Tudor house. He noticed that the shrubbery was kept trim and sculptured.

He walked up the flagstone path to the door. On one of the window panes, he saw a small decal of an American flag. On another was a decal showing the household to be boosters of the Belwyn High School football team.

"All-American family," mused Rabbi Rosen.

He rang the doorbell. No one answered.

He rang the doorbell again.

This time he thought he detected a movement of the drawn windowshade in the window near the door. "Probably that strange old woman is home alone and won't open the door to strangers. Well, I can't fault her for that," thought the rabbi.

He reached into his suit-jacket breast pocket for a note pad and pen. He started a note to Heinrich Hoffmann concerning the sedan.

"Can I help you, sir?"

Rabbi Rosen was startled by the voice with the Teutonic accent that came from behind him. He turned to see a tall, well-preserved elderly gentleman standing in back of him on the doorstep. His first impression was that the man had a military bearing.

"Mr. Hoffmann?" guessed the rabbi.

Pause.

The older man quietly assessed the small, dark-suited figure before him. His eyes especially lingered over the crocheted *kipah* fastened by a bobby pin to the younger man's hair.

"Yes. Do we know each other?"

"I'm Rabbi Rosen of the Belwyn Jewish Center." The rabbi extended his hand. The older man did not shake it. Rabbi Rosen let his hand drop awkwardly to his side.

Very formally, Mr. Hoffmann stated, "I am not Jewish. Some Jewish people may have my family name, but I am not Jewish. You must be looking for some other Hoffmann."

Rabbi Rosen attempted his most cheerful, gracious tone of voice—one he practiced for encounters with congregants who began to annoy him.

"Oh, no. I'm not soliciting for anything. I just came to tell you, in case you didn't know, that your car has been on the synagogue's parking lot since Wednesday night. We need the parking space tonight and tomorrow. Could you please move it?"

"Yes. Some boys who work for me borrowed it. It had mechanical problems. They told me they pulled into that lot off the street and couldn't start it up again. I have been too busy to have it attended to, but I will send the boys to remove it immediately."

"Thank you, Mr. Hoffmann. I appreciate that. Our services begin at 8 P.M. We really do need all the parking spaces. By the way, your car was dented by another car Wednesday night. The police have a license number of the car that hit it, if you should want it."

There was no emotion registered on Hoffmann's face at this news.

"The automobile shall be removed immediately. Good day, Rabbi." Mr. Hoffmann put his key in the door, turned the lock, and went inside abruptly, leaving the rabbi alone on the doorstep.

Rabbi Rosen shrugged his shoulders. He saw all kinds of people in his work. Now he had to go home to his family and make Shabbat. It was the weekend of Russel Himmelfarb's Bar Mitzvah, the Shabbat of the Swastika.

Henkin closed the side door of the Belwyn Jewish Center, turning on the peripheral alarm system. He stared again at the swastika and hated it.

He looked at his wristwatch. There were still three hours in which to go home and prepare the Friday night meal for himself and the Lazarus children. They had chicken last night, so he thought he would cook some turkey parts he had set aside in the refrigerator. He asked himself if he had remembered to take out the two frozen *hallah* breads to defrost.

He was at the synagogue this late in the afternoon to check up on the Himmelfarb's delivery of whisky and wine to the *shul,* an obligatory contribution demanded of all families on the *Shabbos* of the Bar Mitzvah. This was the way the synagogue maintained its supply of liquor for Shabbat morning *Kiddush* and for the *Kiddush* after Friday night services. He was just checking on the Himmelfarbs. The supply of wine was very low. If they had forgotten, he would have to go out and buy some himself for the *shul.* As it was, the Himmelfarbs had remembered, the wine and liquor had been delivered, so Henkin was ready to walk home to make *Shabbos.*

He turned toward the parking lot. In the distance, he could see that a second car had been parked bumper to bumper with the dented sedan that had been there since Wednesday night. Both hoods were open and jumper cables were connecting the batteries of the two vehicles. Two teenaged boys stood by the hoods of the cars. Two others each sat behind the steering wheels.

"Good. They're finally moving that car. Why the

neighbors have to use our lot, I don't know. But what can you say to them? They're all *goyim*. Maybe it's best to let them park there *mipnai darkai sholom,* 'for the sake of good relations.' Now, why the *Jews* need a parking lot for *Shabbos,* that's another question. America. No one can walk a mile. They have to go by machine."

Henkin crossed the narrow street and started walking past the parking lot down Seaville Avenue in the direction of the Lazarus home.

As he got closer to where the boys were standing, he realized that he recognized them. They were there on Thursday night at the Bavarian Steak and Brew! Henkin was sure of it.

That one with the fat lip, he was the one who had hit the young man with the date, then got socked in the mouth himself!

Henkin kept on walking. He could not confront them alone.

His mind, trained in talmudic logic, kept churning. He had suspected those Nazi bastards all along.

10

Ki Vanu Vaharta

Terri and Jeff set the dining room table for the Friday night meal. Each took an end of the white tablecloth and covered the butcher-block top. They set four places. They were both aware of not setting the fifth place at the head of the table. They were both anxious for Sunday to come, and their Dad to return.

In the center of the table, Terri placed the olive-wood *hallah* tray from Israel and its matching breadknife. Jeff brought out the embroidered *hallah* cover that Ruth Lazarus had made so many years before. Together, they brought out the four *kiddush* cups. Henkin's was a huge, antique silver one made in Europe. The three children had their own, each a glass cup set in enameled metal stands of Israeli design.

Henkin puttered about the kitchen. He kept one eye on the turkey parts roasting in the oven, the other on his spearing of gefilte fish pieces as he thrust a fork into the jar. He arranged his catch on lettuce beds on four small plates.

Robert came downstairs. He was freshly show-ered, his hair blown dry. The house smelled "*Shabbos-dig*," as Henkin would put it. The aroma of the roast turkey mingled with the fragrance of freshly baked *hallah.* No other dinner time of the week ever seemed the same. Friday night dinner always permeated the atmosphere of the entire house.

Robert fell to helping. He brought the still warm *hallah* breads to the table, placed them on the tray, and covered them lovingly with his mother's *hallah* cover. He brought the sweet concord wine from the refrigerator and filled the four cups.

He was still feeling rotten over his breakup with Lauryn, but he masked his feelings in front of Henkin and his little brother and sister. He *was* their older brother, the one they looked up to, a kind of substitute father when Dad was out of town. So he held in his personal feelings, though he sometimes could help Terri and Jeff to solve their more dramatic emotional problems.

Robert considered confiding in Henkin. He had discovered a new dimension in Henkin since the story told on Thursday night. But Henkin was grumpily dishing out gefilte fish, and it hardly seemed the right time.

Robert looked over at Terri. She was sniping at an unusually passive Jeff. "How many times do you have to be told?" she demanded. "Knives go next to the plate, *then* spoons!"

Robert thought to himself, "Am I projecting my own mood on everyone else, or are we all feeling miserable?"

Henkin davened *Minhah* from a small *siddur* with a vinyl cover, while standing by the kitchen counter. Friday night services at the Belwyn Jewish Center started at 8 P.M. all year long. They were designed to be after-dinner services, followed by tea and cake at the *Oneg Shabbat.* So they were *Maariv* or evening services. At this time of year, by Shabbat *Korah,* it did not get dark until well after eight. Henkin had formed

Henkin closed the prayer book. It was a signal for Terri to light the Sabbath candles.

the habit of davening *Minhah* or afternoon services before dinner. He also let Terri light the candles before the meal, making Shabbat early. It was another of his compromises with Jewish life in America.

Henkin closed the prayer book. It was a signal for Terri to light the Sabbath candles. Terri tied a kerchief to her head. While Henkin and the boys stood in a half-circle behind her, she covered her eyes with her hands and recited the blessing. When she uncovered her eyes at the end of the blessing, she turned to the boys and Henkin and greeted them, "*Shabbat Shalom.*" They answered, "*Shabbat Shalom.*" Terri kissed Henkin on the forehead. Each of her brothers kissed her on the cheek.

They all took their places at the dining room table. Together they sang *Shalom Aleichem*. Henkin recited the *Kiddush* in a kind of undertone, pausing to let the children join in the melody at the words "*ki vanu vaharta.*"

Next, there was a slow march to the kitchen sink in single file after Henkin, where each in order of age washed hands, pouring water from a special cup with two handles and mumbling the "*netilat yadayim*" blessing. Back at the dining room table, Robert made "*Ha-motzi*" over the two *hallah* loaves and tore a piece of bread for each person. Jeff brought the plates of gefilte fish in from the kitchen. They sat eating in silence.

Silence was the unusual part of this Friday meal. Robert was convinced that something—and not necessarily the same thing—was troubling each of them.

Robert couldn't take it any longer. He stopped picking at his fish, which he never liked that much anyway, and blurted out, "Okay. What's bothering everybody? Terri first."

Terri looked down at her empty plate. "I got a hundred on my biology test."

"And that makes you upset?" asked Robert. "You went into that test complaining that you were going to flunk!"

"Yeah, like you always do," said Jeff. "I knew you'd get a hundred. You always do."

"I don't understand it," said Robert. "You studied hard. You were well-prepared. You got a hundred. Why are you upset? You should be happy."

"Yeah, sure," said Terri, fighting back tears. "You really *don't* understand, do you?" She could see that Jeff was tapping his pointer finger several times on his temple as he clandestinely smiled at Robert.

Henkin said to Terri, "To be a good student is usually an honor. To be honored is also to be envied. To be envied is often to be hated. There is hope of healing every hatred, except the hatred that comes of envy."

"Thanks a lot," said Terri. "What should I do? I want to do well in school, but I don't want to be different. I want to be liked."

"You mean everyone doesn't like you?" probed Robert, trying to convince Terri that she was exaggerating.

"Well, Mary Beth likes me, of course. But there are a whole group of girls in my grade who really make me feel resented. I'm not imagining it, Robbie."

"Maybe it would help if you weren't so obvious about yourself. You *are* a grind," suggested Robert. "Get good grades, but don't be so pushy. Don't call so much attention to yourself."

"How can I help that, Robbie?" Terri said, defensively. "The teachers single me out and hold me up to the class as a model."

"Torpedo the others," blurted Jeff. "If you're better at school, *be* better! They're jealous, like Henkin said. Those who like you are your real friends. The others aren't worth it anyway. If they were smarter and friendlier, they could learn from you. If they're jealous dopes, they deserve to be stupid! Right, Henkin?"

"*Or lagoyim*," said Henkin. "The Jews throughout history are meant to be a light to the nations. Some people like darkness better. Light hurts their eyes. They hate especially the ones holding the torch. There's nothing you can do, Terri. You're a bright girl, a pretty girl, a talented girl. You have to be true to yourself. One day they may profit from your brightness, your talent. Then, maybe, they'll understand. Maybe they won't. It's the history of the Jewish people."

"Oh, you and the Jewish people," sobbed Terri. "Why do I even have to be Jewish?"

Henkin looked rebuffed, so Terri said, "I'm sorry, Henkin. But, you really don't understand. I'm not history. I'm a kid in high school."

"Maybe you're right," said Henkin. "But it is important for you to keep doing well. The rest can't always be helped. It's no solution to stop doing well. Trust me."

"It still doesn't solve my problem. I'm still not happy." Terri got up and collected the finished and the never-to-be-finished plates of gefilte fish. She took them into the kitchen, scraped the refuse into the garbage, and put the dirty dishes into the *fleishig* plastic washtub sitting in the sink.

She transferred the turkey parts from the roasting pan into a large serving platter. Then she noticed that Henkin had opened a can of cling peaches for a side dish.

"Meat and fruit," thought Terri. "Henkin and his light to the nations. The old man must have been the inventor of *nouvelle cuisine*. Still, he's probably right about the peaches going with roast turkey. He's probably right about a lot of things."

In the dining room, it was Jeff's turn.

"I got locked in my locker at school today."

"You got what?" Robert wasn't sure whether to laugh or not.

"I got shoved and pushed into my locker by the guy I told you about yesterday, Robbie. I wasn't looking for trouble. He was standing by my locker when I needed to go to it. Lewis got me out."

Henkin showed real concern. "Jeff, by 'the guy,' do you mean the same guy who beat you up yesterday?"

Jeff nodded. He still wasn't sure how much he wanted to tell Henkin.

"This is 'the guy' who desecrated your *Maftir* booklet with God's name written in it and called you a dirty Jew while beating you?" asked Henkin, sounding like a lawyer. "Tell me who this 'guy' is. Something must be done. We don't make the mistake of standing around waiting any more."

"Well, maybe Jeff *should* go to the principal and tell the principal his problem," said Robert.

"I have my own idea," said Jeff. "I'll handle it my way. The guy had a fat lip today. *Somebody* must have punched his face. Maybe, with help, we can keep him in fat lips until he *stops* bothering people."

Henkin's concern seemed to deepen. "What is this guy's name, Jeffrey?"

Jeff looked at Robert, and said, "I want to handle it my way, Henkin."

Henkin could see it was no use to press further. But something about Jeff's story rang a bell with him: the guy with the "fat lip."

Terri came to the table with the turkey platter, decorated with the cling peaches. The rest of the meal went by in silence.

Robert cleared the dishes from the table. In the kitchen, he poured Henkin's special concentrated liquid tea and hot water from a large electric urn. The urn kept water hot all through Shabbat, and Henkin always brewed the strong concentrate to make tea for Sabbath. One by one, Robert brought the four teacups to the table.

Finally, Henkin broke the silence. "Let's *bentsch*," he said, "or we'll be late for *shul*."

They hastily said the Grace after Meals. Henkin managed to do it all, while the Lazarus children did varying amounts of it. The table was quickly cleared; the dishes were left to soak in the tub in the sink. Ties and jackets were added to the boys' attire. Terri went to her room in sweatshirt and designer jeans and emerged wearing a blouse and skirt.

They walked, together with Henkin, slowly, up Seaville Avenue to the Belwyn Jewish Center.

11
At Services

Friday Night. 8:05 P.M.

Rabbi Rosen sat on his velvet-covered chair by the Holy Ark on the *bimah,* watching the congregants enter the sanctuary. There was some discernable buzzing about the swastika and the menacing slogan painted on the door facing the parking lot. The buzzing was not loud, however, for not many people had shown up for services.

Rabbi Rosen looked out to the pews and nodded his head and smiled to some of the congregants. But he was disappointed. Here it was, 8:05 already, the first Friday since the swastika painting, after an article about the synagogue was in *Newsday,* the weekend of a Bar Mitzvah, and they still did not have a *minyan.*

There were, it was true, about twenty-five people scattered among the pews that held two hundred or so. But, among all the women and children, counting himself and the cantor, there were only nine males above the age of Bar Mitzvah.

Russel and his family were seated in the first row, except for Vivian Himmelfarb who was animatedly talking and gesturing with B. B. Braverman at the rear entrance to the sanctuary. B. B. had a conciliatory look on his face, and it looked as if he could not get a word in edgewise. Occasionally, Mrs. Himmelfarb glanced in the rabbi's direction, then went back to jabbering and gesticulating.

The rabbi noticed that Henkin was present. He could always count on Henkin. The Lazarus kids were with him. Good. At least Robert counted toward the *minyan*. Russel Himmelfarb and his father and one grandfather were also part of the count. Thank God for a Bar Mitzvah weekend! B. B. Braverman and another man brought the count to nine. Nine out of ten.

The congregation's custom did not include women in the basic count for a *minyan*. Most of the time, it was a moot point, because there were more than enough people and *nobody* had to be counted. Rabbi Rosen always said that he gave women "the higher numbers, from eleven upwards." Tonight was one of those occasional, aggravating nights when the tension about women's rights came to the fore, all because the men didn't live up to their responsibilities.

At least by holding out for ten adult males, Rabbi Rosen reasoned, he had a chance of getting twenty-six people at this service instead of twenty-five. In either case, it was a terrible turnout. The rabbi was annoyed even before the service began.

It was getting late. Rabbi Rosen decided to start services now, hoping that a tenth adult male would materialize before the congregation reached the *"Barchu."*

They started services with *"Yedid Nefesh,"* an additional hymn which Rabbi Rosen had printed up and pasted to the back leaf of the congregation's prayer books. Usually, he would call a child up to the cantor's lectern to lead this hymn. This evening, Rabbi Rosen made a point of calling up a *girl*. That would show them.

While the congregation sang the hymn in unison, B. B. Braverman, happy to be relieved of Vivian Himmelfarb who had taken her seat on the front row, stood by the sanctuary door, on the lookout for the tenth man.

A black youth, well over six feet tall, entered the sanctuary at *"Lecha Dodi."* He wore a small, crocheted *kipah* pinned to his hair. The name, "Moshe," in Hebrew letters was neatly worked into the pattern.

The young man towered over B. B. Braverman, who was no small man himself. The rabbi could make out the black man's greeting of *"Shabbat shalom,"* and his hasty handshake with the amazed *shul* president. The rabbi smiled inwardly.

He followed with his eyes as the black youth walked confidently down the center aisle to an almost filled pew. He sat down amidst a silent ripple of furtive glances and tense nudges and strange smiles. Rabbi Rosen took mental note of the newcomer's apparent familiarity with synagogue services. The youth immediately found the place in the siddur and began davening with fluency.

B. B. Braverman sat down next to the young man. He seemed to be questioning the stranger for a few moments. B. B. then got up from his seat, walked to the *bimah,* and sat in his president's seat beside the rabbi.

B. B. leaned over to the rabbi and whispered, "Well, do we count him in the minyan?"

"Why do you ask?" The rabbi was playing a little.

"C'mon, Rabbi. *You* know."

"No, I don't know."

"Is he really Jewish? I couldn't get much information out of him. He told me I was interrupting his davening."

"B. B., he's right. Let me ask you something. The first time *you* showed up at this *shul,* did anyone ask you if *you* were Jewish?"

"No. But this is different."

"Why? Because he's black?"

"You have to admit, Rabbi. It does raise questions. The presumption is that Jews are white. A black Jew has to be asked how he *became* Jewish. Conversion? Was it 'legit'? C'mon, Rabbi, you know what I mean."

"Okay. I'll concede you have a point, B. B. But look at him davening over there. *Halevai,* "it should only be" that the rest of the congregation could daven that well. He's obviously had some real Jewish training. Anyway, until we know differently, he's considered Jewish and counts to the *minyan.* And, tonight we really need him."

"I could still slip away quietly and make a telephone call for another man."

"Not on Shabbat, you won't," said the rabbi. "The black man counts, and that's final."

Russel did an adequate job of chanting the Friday night *Kiddush.* Rabbi Rosen felt a little easier. Russel would probably pull tomorrow off reasonably well, too.

The rabbi informed the group that his morning sermon would be about the swastika on the synagogue door. He also expressed his amazement that more congregants had not shown up for Friday services; curiosity, at least, should bring a turnout.

After the singing of *Yigdal,* led by a cute row of small children chanting alternate verses from the *bimah,* the rabbi blessed the congregation and invited everyone to take part in the *Oneg Shabbat* sponsored by the Himmelfarb family in honor of Russel's becoming a Bar Mitzvah.

As the rabbi stepped down from the *bimah* and out the sanctuary door to the ballroom for the *Oneg Shabbat,* he was stopped by Henkin and the Lazarus kids.

"*Shabbat shalom,* Rabbi," said Robert. "We stand by you about leaving the swastika up."

"Thanks, Robert. I know there are people who think I should have had it removed for the Bar Mitzvah. Terri, *Shabbat shalom.* It's nice to see you in *shul.*"

Terri looked down. She didn't come to services as often as her brothers. She found them boring.

"Well, the swastika made me feel like I had to show some solidarity, if you know what I mean," said Terri.

"I do," said Rabbi Rosen. "I hoped that more people would feel that way about it."

"Are there any leads in the case yet?" asked Jeff, trying to move the conversation along.

"Well, the police are still vague, but I suspect that they've located the driver of that yellow car."

"Big deal," said Jeff. "We know who that was, too. Besides, we don't think he did it. The cops are so dumb."

"What do you mean?" asked the rabbi.

"There are *real* Nazis in Belwyn," said Henkin with his usual blunt impatience.

"Henkin, don't get carried away," said the rabbi. "I think it's youthful vandalism that we can nip in the bud. We'll bring the kids who did it into court and they'll be sentenced to some kind of community service work. That's what it was in other synagogues with the same kind of thing."

"Rabbi Rosen," said Henkin, "you're a nice young man with liberal feelings. You are also very naive. I am telling you that there is a Nazi living here in Belwyn. He heads something called the White America Party. And he uses an assumed name. But I know him. I would never forget him."

"Henkin. Do you have proof? That's a serious charge you're making."

Robert hastily interjected. "We don't have proof."

"What's the man's name?" the rabbi asked Henkin.

"He calls himself Heinrich Hoffmann. He owns the Bavarian Steak and Brew restaurant."

"Heinrich Hoffmann?" The rabbi's eyes widened. "The police gave me that name. He is the owner of the car that was on the parking lot that night, the one that got dented."

The Lazarus children looked at each other and at Henkin.

"I'll walk over to the Fifth Precinct after services tomorrow," said Rabbi Rosen. "The police should at least know your suspicions. Will you come with me?"

"Sure, Rabbi." It was Jeff who answered. Robert and Terri nodded in agreement.

"We'll leave after services tomorrow. And after I spend a little time at Shabbat lunch with my family. Meanwhile, keep everything to yourselves. Promise? There's no real proof as yet."

"Absolutely, Rabbi," said Robert.

Henkin seemed triumphant. He had made his point.

"They're waiting for us at the *Oneg*. We'd better hurry into the ballroom." Rabbi Rosen led the way.

The congregants stood around three large tables in the ballroom. The tables were laden with trays of cakes, large pitchers of hot tea, and settings for ten. Three other tables were empty, a nagging reminder to Rabbi Rosen of the poor turnout.

The cantor led the group in singing "*Shalom Alei-chem*," after which the rabbi asked Russel Himmelfarb to recite the blessing over the fancy little cakes ordered in honor of the Bar Mitzvah.

Russel mistakenly finished the blessing with the words "*boray p'ri ha-gafen*." In unison, everyone corrected him with "*boray minay mezonot*," but they beamed at him with joy, anyway. Russel bit into his cherry tart and everybody sat down to tea and cake.

Rabbi Rosen made certain to sit beside the young black Jew. He wanted to meet him and to introduce him to others in the congregation.

"Shabbat shalom," the rabbi said, extending his hand in greeting. "I'm Rabbi Rosen."

"Shabbat shalom. Kor'im li Moshe Williams."

"Ah, you speak Hebrew, Moshe."

"I just came back from a year in Israel. I played on an Israeli basketball team. Semi-pro. They all are over there."

"Great. *Na'im meod.* It's good to meet you. Do you live in Belwyn?"

"My parents recently moved in. I'm living in Brooklyn now, on Eastern Parkway."

"Well, your parents are certainly welcome to come to synagogue here."

"I don't think so," said the young man.

"Why not?" asked Rabbi Rosen defensively, beginning to worry that maybe his congregants made the young black Jew feel uncomfortable or unwelcome.

"We're Orthodox and this is a Conservative synagogue. I couldn't tell from the outside."

"Well, your parents are always welcome should they come. There are no Orthodox synagogues within walking distance from here. And, we're a very traditional congregation. They might like it."

"I don't think so," the young giant said again.

"Well, where are you going to daven tomorrow? We're really the most traditional synagogue in the area."

"I guess I'll come back here tomorrow, if I don't just daven with my father at home."

"Well, if you do come tomorrow, I'd like to invite

you to have Shabbat lunch with me and my wife and kids at my home after services. It's just down the street."

"Sorry, I can't."

Rabbi Rosen smiled uneasily. In a half-joking voice he said, "You trust my *kashrut,* of course, don't you? You know you've got nothing to worry about."

"Well, that's just it. My family and I have a rule. We don't eat at the homes of Conservative Jews. I suppose it leaves us open for hard feelings at times, but that's just the way it is."

CRA-A-A-SH!

All heads instinctively turned in the direction of the nerve-wracking sound of glass shattering. A brick hurled from outside burst through a ballroom window and crossed the room like a cannon shot. It sailed close by the heads of those seated at the Himmelfarb table and hit the carpet a foot short of where the rabbi and Moshe were sitting. A slightly different angle of trajectory, and the brick could have randomly killed either Moshe or the rabbi.

They all rose from their seats. Two men ran to the synagogue's main entrance near the ballroom to see if they might catch someone running away outside. The rest gathered around the brick.

It was wrapped in brown paper, tied with string. Rabbi Rosen picked it up and untied the string. There was writing on the paper, printed in felt tip pen.

The two men who had run to the door came back. They hadn't seen anybody outside.

Rabbi Rosen read the paper out loud. "Zionist pigs. We'll finish the job Hitler started. Long live Palestine!"

The congregants were silent. Then, suddenly, Vivian Himmelfarb shrieked.

"First, a swastika on the door. Now, a broken window in the ballroom. My Bar Mitzvah is *ruined*! And, Rabbi Rosen," her eyes narrowed as she pointed her finger, "it's all your fault!"

12

Rabbi Rosen's Sermon

Saturday Morning. 9:30 A.M.

Robert Lazarus sat down in a pew near the middle of the sanctuary beside his sister Terri. All three Lazarus children had arrived for Shabbat morning services about a half-hour after the *Birchot Ha-sha-har,* the early morning prayers, began.

Jeff was invited to Russel's Bar Mitzvah ceremony. He found his way to a row of chattering boys and girls his age who were also invited. Some of these kids were in Jeff's Hebrew school class. Others were non-Jewish friends from Belwyn Junior High.

Robert glanced around. He smiled to himself. The number of worshippers present by 9:30 A.M. on a Saturday morning was true to an unwritten law of synagogue attendance Robert had discovered during his years of regular *shul* going.

A Shabbat morning service at the Belwyn Jewish Center formally began at nine o'clock. However, there was usually little more than a minimum *minyan* present at nine—the rabbi, the cantor, and some of the older men like Henkin who were also the mainstay of the weekday morning services.

The first half hour of Saturday services was made up of morning blessings, psalms, and other little tidbits of liturgy. It was one of the congregants who customarily led this part of the services from the pulpit. And the whole thing sounded like mumbling in code.

The cantor took over at *"Shochein Ad,"* about nine thirty in the morning. The services immediately switched to more respectable singing. Now began the recognizable tunes and responses.

The Bar Mitzvah boy and his immediate family were also expected to be in *shul* in time for the 9:00 A.M. start of services. The Bar Mitzvah boy sat on a pulpit chair near the cantor's seat. The boy's family sat in the front row pews on the cantor's side of the center aisle.

There was only one other class of people in the sanctuary by 9:00 A.M. on a Saturday morning. These were the gentile guests of the Bar Mitzvah. The gentiles were understandably unaware of Jewish practice. They were the ones who actually *believed* the printed Bar Mitzvah invitations which announced "Services beginning at 9:00 A.M." Except for maybe the Bar Mitzvah boy and his family, the gentiles were the ones who looked lost and bewildered during the rapid humming in Hebrew.

Between nine thirty and ten, the second wave of Sabbath morning regulars began arriving. Most of the *Jewish* guests got there by ten. Ten was the civilized time to make an appearance. By ten, the Torah scroll was laid on the cantor's lectern. By ten, the rabbi's sermon was about to begin. Besides, it would be a good ten forty-five, or eleven, before the Bar Mitzvah boy himself would be "on."

Robert was waiting impatiently to hear what Rabbi Rosen would say in his sermon. When he and

Terri and Jeff arrived at nine thirty, the Back Hallway Caucus was grumbling negatively about the rabbi's "wisdom" and his motives for leaving the swastika up and for having a news item printed in *Newsday*. The Back Hallway Caucus was made up of five or so gentlemen who spent every Saturday service outside the rear sanctuary doors faithfully gossiping and debating synagogue politics. The Caucus blamed the *rabbi* for calling attention to the synagogue, and, consequently, for the brick thrown through the ballroom window on Friday night.

Terri was incensed at the talk. She personally agreed with the rabbi's decision. So did Robert and Jeff. Robert had to restrain Terri from bawling the men out. He grabbed her by the arm and escorted her into the sanctuary.

At ten, on schedule, Rabbi Rosen began his sermon. "This Shabbat, we read from the *Sidra* of Korah," commenced the rabbi in a casual tone of voice.

"Every week, the same opening," groused a man sitting directly behind Robert. "This Shabbat we read from the Sidra of . . . Some rabbi, all he ever talks about is the Torah reading."

Terri turned in her seat and said, "Shush!"

Rabbi Rosen paid no attention. "But this Shabbat, with your permission, I shall not talk about the Torah reading."

He paused, and swept the entire congregation with his eyes. The rabbi brought himself up to his full height on the carpet-covered block on which he had to stand in order to see the congregation over his lectern. Being short carried its own problems.

"I shall speak this morning to the issue of the swastika painted on our door last Wednesday night. I speak with heavy heart about this desecration of our holy synagogue. I shall tell you why we chose to react as we did. I shall share with you what we as a Jewish community hope to accomplish by not remaining silent. I shall speak this morning directly to your, no, to *our* Jewish souls.

"First, I would like to remind my fellow Jews that there are all kinds of signs and symbols.

"This Shabbat, for instance, we are observing the Bar Mitzvah celebration of Russel Himmelfarb. As a *sign* that Russel has achieved the age of religious responsibility, he will shortly be called to the Torah and then chant his *haftorah*. As an adult Jewish male, he comes under the *mitzvah* of *tefillin*, tied as a *sign* upon the hand and as frontlets between the eyes. Russel will be reminded every time he puts on his *tefillin* of the *mitzvot*, the commandments, of the Torah.

"In fact, we do not don *tefillin* at Sabbath services because the Sabbath *itself* is a *sign*, as the Torah says 'ot hi l'olam,' an eternal sign between God and the children of Israel that in six days God made heaven and earth and on the seventh day He rested.

"Our religious signs are potent symbols of the heritage of Torah which was handed to us by our fathers and which we hand down to our children through all the generations.

"The swastika is another kind of sign, a sign darker than the black spray paint on our white synagogue door. The swastika, too, is a potent symbol to us Jews. It stands for perhaps the ugliest persecution of Jews in all of Jewish history. This was what was done to us by the German Third Reich—and its accomplices—a generation ago. The swastika will always remind us of those forces that single out the Jew for destruction, that seek to wipe the Jews from the face of the earth.

"The swastika painted on our synagogue door is a sign that just can't be ignored.

"I know that some even now disagree with my decision to leave the desecration up and to have it publicized in the press. We have since had a brick thrown through a ballroom window. Whether it was by the same people or a *new* incident brought on by the publicity, I do not myself know at this time.

"The brick thrown last night was wrapped in a paper with the message 'Long live Palestine!' Today, there are malicious villians who declare that Zionism is racism, who want to destroy the miracle that is the State of Israel. They claim they wish to help the Palestinian Arabs. Yet, they attack the entire Jewish people, everywhere in the world, with the same lies and distortions that have always marked anti-Semites. And now, our synagogue in Belwyn, Long Island, has been touched by this madness.

"The brick and the swastika are related. They both spell irrational hatred against Jews. The ideologies and high-sounding reasons are tacked on later. And, ironically, the pro-Arabs talk about Jews as Nazis! So anti-Semitism has its own perverse thinking.

"But we live in America. We have the precious gift of religious and ethnic liberty. We have laws that protect us. We, as a Jewish congregation, must respond to attacks through legal means. While the broken window will be repaired once Shabbat is over, the swastika will remain until we have exhausted every legal means to find who did it and bring that person or persons to justice.

"Some might argue that the event was just youthful vandalism; therefore, insignificant. Even if that proves to be the case—as I think it may very well be— the vandals will learn through this the gravity of the symbol of their prank. They will be forced to study about the Holocaust, and to sand and repaint the door by court order. We must speak out and act to stop such heinous thinking and action, and to ensure that America remains a land of liberty.

"I am sorry that these events of the past week have intruded on the Himmelfarb *simhah* of Russel's becoming a Bar Mitzvah. But part of Russel's growth into adult responsibility is his casting his lot with the fate of the Jewish community—for good times, or for times when being Jewish can be uncomfortable. This Shabbat, Russel is truly becoming a man, as he joins our Jewish community in taking a stand for Jewish rights and Jewish dignity."

Vivian Himmelfarb shifted uncomfortably on the front row seat throughout the rabbi's sermon. She was convinced that the Bar Mitzvah was ruined by the spray-painted, broken-windowed condition of the *shul*. What would people think of her as a hostess? It was like inviting people to a party in your home and not picking up the newspapers and discarded clothing on the furniture before the guests arrived.

Vivian turned from time to time to see the reaction of the California people, especially that of her cousin Gladys, her arch-rival. Gladys had her eyes riveted on the young rabbi throughout his sermon.

Russel made the same mistakes in chanting his *haftorah* that he made in every rehearsal. He added a few that Henkin had never heard him make before.

Rabbi Rosen said that Russel had done a wonderful job and that everyone in his family and in the congregation was proud of him. Indeed, everyone was. Russel chanting a *haftorah* was not altogether unlike a trained seal playing "Yankee Doodle" on a row of bicycle horns. You don't criticize the seal's musical abilities. It's a marvel that the seal can play at all.

After services, at the *Kiddush,* Rabbi Rosen went over to where Vivian Himmelfarb stood talking to her California cousin Gladys.

"*Mazel tov,* Vivian," offered the rabbi. "Russel certainly came through."

"Thank you, Rabbi," said Vivian. "The services were beautiful. I'd like you to meet my cousin, Gladys, from California."

"How do you do? *Shabbat shalom.*"

"Nice meeting you, Rabbi," said Gladys. "Stick to your guns about the swastika. I like a rabbi who's an activist." She smiled broadly.

"Thank you," said the rabbi, a bit taken aback. "Vivian, I'm sorry that I can't stay for the reception. I'm going to take a walk to the Fifth Precinct this afternoon to report the brick-throwing incident and to check on the progress of the swastika case."

"I understand, Rabbi. Sorry you can't stay."

When Rabbi Rosen was out of earshot, Gladys turned to Vivian and cooed, "What a dynamic young rabbi you have. He's just marvelous. And what an exciting Bar Mitzvah you have thrown, Vivian. A social action Bar Mitzvah. It's the most interesting Bar Mitzvah in the family in years."

"Well, I've got to stand up as a Jew, you know."

"I just love your rabbi. Such fire. Such sincerity. Such charisma. I'd like to take him back to California to spark a few people at *our* temple."

"Don't you dare. We all love him here."

"And he's so cute, too."

13
A Wolf in Sheep's Clothing

Sausage and scrambled eggs sizzled in the divided skillet on the gas range. The aroma of fried pork wafted from the kitchen up to the second-story bedroom of the Tudor house on Sage Street. It seemed that the anticipation of Saturday morning brunch was taking a ride up the electric elevator chair fitted several years ago to the staircase of the tidy little home.

The old woman opened her eyes and tried to sit up in bed. She couldn't. So she waited.

She turned her eyes to a photograph in a gilded frame on her night table. Staring back at her were the smiling and confident faces of a beautiful blonde girl, her tall husband in his handsome military uniform, and their eight-year-old son in the light-colored uniform of his youth group.

"We were at the top of the world then," she thought, as she had thought a million times while looking at that photograph. "And it all came crashing down. Little Wilhelm, killed in the bombing of Dresden. The defeat. Fleeing to America. And, now, to end my life like this: an old lady with hardening of the arteries, waited on hand and foot by my husband. I can't even go to the bathroom by myself anymore."

Downstairs, in the kitchen, two plates of sausage and eggs, two glasses of orange juice, two cups of coffee, two sets of napkins and silverware, and a pitcher of cream, were laid out on a bed tray with all the precision and expertise of a restauranteur.

The husband carried the tray up the stairs. He paused at the open bedroom door and smiled tenderly. *"Guten Morgen."*

Though an old man himself, the husband looked younger than his years. He still stood straight and tall. His full shock of white hair was cropped short, 1940s style, with a high part on the right side of his head. His glasses frames were stylish, and his plaid sportshirt, flannel slacks, and cordovan loafers added to the impression of a person still concerned about appearances, even at home.

He set the tray down on a chair by the bed. With strong arms, he gently lifted his wife to a sitting position and fluffed some pillows for her back. After the tray was placed so that it straddled her lap over the covers, he sat down on the bedside chair and began to share the meal he had made.

The woman looked at him. He was still so handsome after all these years. But she knew something was troubling him.

"What's bothering you, dearest?"

"Don't worry. I can take care of it."

"I am worried," she said. "ever since that rabbi called yesterday. I have a feeling of dread."

"Don't worry. I can take care of it, I told you."

"The Jews know, don't they? They always seem to know and spoil everything." She reached for his hand. He held hers with his.

'I don't know what they know and I don't care. They are the same here as there. Always getting in the way of our lives."

"I have always been so careful. I kept to myself.

Now I'm sick and must keep to myself anyway. I have no choice."

The man nodded compassionately.

She said, "But you, dearest, with your political activities. You expose yourself too much. I always knew it would mean trouble in the end. They still control the world, you know, even here."

"That's why my activities are so important. A man must do what is right. The Jewish problem is stronger than ever. Some day the world will thank us."

"I'm frightened. In America, Jews are powerful. They get what they want."

"I can take care of it."

"The rabbi calling the house on the phone, and then actually standing on our doorstep—that worries me. It's an omen."

"Nonsense. I'm not concerned by some small rabbi. I only worry about an old Jew that came to the restaurant Thursday night during our meeting. I think he may have recognized me. A stupid old man to look at, but perhaps shrewd. He started a fight."

"My God. They must know. Why else would he have come there? He must have told the rabbi."

"Not necessarily. The two things may be totally separate. But I am furious at those young dolts we recruited for the Party. They borrowed my car last Wednesday for a rally of Solidarity with the Palestinians. Then they went and painted a swastika on the synagogue down on Seaville Avenue. *Then,* they couldn't get the car started again, so they abandoned it on the parking lot there. Dolts. No one ordered the swastika painting. It could ruin everything. It was premature. I could kill those morons. Every noble cause is wrecked by the inferior dolts that are recruited to do the work."

"What about the old Jew? That worries me more than the rabbi. Are you sure he recognized you?"

"I will take care of that, too," said the man. "I have seen him before in town. He goes often to that synagogue."

"Be careful, dearest. You are all that I have left in this world."

"I will always protect you and care for you. I promise you, I can take care of these problems."

"Kurt?"

"*Liebchen*, it must always be *Heinrich*, even at home. Don't let your guard down now, after all these years. And don't bother yourself. I will take care of it."

"You are my one and only."

He picked up the tray and left the bedroom. With his foot, he closed the door behind him. He paused in the hall to think, then took the tray downstairs to the kitchen. Setting it down, he picked up the telephone and called the Fifth Precinct.

14
The Short Arm of the Law

Saturday Afternoon.

After Shabbat lunch with Henkin, Robert and Terri made ready to go to the rabbi's house on Seaville Avenue. The three would then pick up Jeff at Russel's Bar Mitzvah reception and walk the two miles or so to the Fifth Precinct station.

"I want to go with you," said Henkin.

"It's too far a walk," Robert answered. Terri put both her hands on Henkin's shoulders from behind his chair and kissed him on the top of his *kipah.*

"You'll tell the police everything I told you? You'll tell them that Hoffmann is really that Nazi Kurt Hammerstein?"

"We'll tell them," said Terri.

"Well, at least we'll have the rabbi with us. He'll handle the police," said Robert.

"It's not suspicion, children. It's fact."

Henkin seemed edgy.

"You told the rabbi. He'll know what to say."

"I'll clear the table. I imagine that old Henkin is not good for anything today except to take his *Shabbos* nap until *Minhah* service at the *shul.*"

"Oh, Henkin," said Terri, "you're plenty good."

"So, hurry to the rabbi. Do you want to spend all *Shabbos* talking to an old man?"

"See you later, Henkin." Robert pulled Terri out the front door.

Rabbi Rosen was finishing lunch with his wife and his children when Robert and Terri knocked at his door. He brought them in. Neither of them wanted dessert, but they pulled up chairs to the table and listened as the rabbi and his family chanted the Grace. Then Rabbi Rosen kissed his wife and children, and together with Robert and Terri, he walked on to the Belwyn Jewish Center.

In the ballroom of the synagogue, the broken window was largely forgotten by the crowd of guests at Russel's Bar Mitzvah reception.

A hired master of ceremonies spoke into the microphone and asked everyone to go back to the tables. It was time for the "traditional" ceremony of placing flags on the Bar Mitzvah cake. Honored members of the Himmelfarb family were each to be called to place a little Israeli flag on the cake.

When Rabbi Rosen, Robert, and Terri arrived, the M.C. was announcing, "And, now . . . Aunt Gertie from Mineola. Please step up, darling."

An elderly woman with a walker rose and ambled toward the cake.

Robert came over to Jeff. "Let's go," he said, "we're on our way to the police station now."

Jeff, his eyes fixed on Aunt Gertie and the cake, said, "Just a minute, Robbie. I want to see this. It's the best part."

"Are you for real?"

"Oh, all right. I'm coming."

The rabbi left the ballroom with the three Lazarus kids.

Aunt Gertie from Mineola planted her little flag with both hands a layer and a half deep into the Bar Mitzvah cake. Russel's father helped her up, getting blue and white icing all over his designer suit.

Officer Oates happened to be at the front desk of the police precinct.

"Rabbi Rosen and Company, I see," he said with a wink.

"Officer Oates," Rabbi Rosen answered directly. "I have another incident to report. I couldn't telephone because it is the Jewish Sabbath."

"Rabbi, you came at the right time," said Oates. "We've got a brand new department in the County Police to investigate and, hopefully, to prosecute these acts of vandalism against churches and synagogues. It happens to churches, too, you know. The new department is also going after acts of vandalism and bigotry against private property and individual citizens, too. We have a detective on the inspector level heading it. He's in the building now. I'll phone up for you. It's Inspector Grady, second floor, third door down from the stairs."

The rabbi and the three kids knocked on the door and entered Inspector Grady's little office.

Grady seemed a warm, friendly man. As he rose from his desk to welcome his arrivals, he showed himself to be about the minimum height for a cop, with a beer drinker's belly protruding over the belt of suit slacks purchased in leaner days. He had a receding hairline.

He shook hands all around, pointed to chairs in front of his desk, then sat down again.

117

"Rabbi Rosen," the inspector began, "the swastika painted on your synagogue is my first official case. I was waiting to call on you Monday."

He opened the only file folder on his desk. "I want you to know we have already brought in someone for questioning. Yesterday afternoon, in fact."

"May we know who it was?" asked the rabbi.

"Well, not really. We're not ready yet. It was a preliminary questioning." The inspector quickly closed the file folder when he saw Jeff reading the report, even though it was upside down for him.

"We know who you brought in, anyway," countered Jeff, as he leaned forward on his crossed arms resting on the desk top. "Brian Epstein. We don't think he did it."

Robert tapped Jeff lightly on the ankle with the side of his foot, signalling Jeff to be quiet. He had forgotten that Jeff's ankle was still tender from Thursday's beating.

"Ouch, Robbie. What did you do that for?"

Robert glowered at him. Jeff backed down.

"Since you already seem to know," confided the detective, "we have no solid evidence against him either. Of course, we can place the Epstein boy at the scene that evening."

"Yes," said Robert. "He admitted that to me in school on Thursday. He was there. And he was frightened. That was all I could find out."

"He seems a high-strung kid," offered the inspector. "A Jew for Jesus. No offense, Rabbi, but while I think his belief in Jesus is admirable, he should become a Catholic. Know what I mean? These cult kids are usually off the wall. I couldn't get much out of him, and, so far, he's the only one we can place at the scene that night."

Rabbi Rosen spoke up. "I have another hypothesis I would like to sound out with you, if I may."

"By all means," responded Grady.

"Well," the rabbi went on, "it almost frightens me to bring this up. But there was a sedan on the parking lot Wednesday night that was damaged by the yellow car, according to a witness from across the street."

"That's in the report. But neighborhood cars are often parked overnight in the temple lot, as I understand."

"True, but this one was still on the lot on *Friday!* We needed the spaces this Sabbath, so I traced the owner's name through the precinct, to let him know about the car and to ask him to move it."

"And?"

"The owner's name is Heinrich Hoffmann."

"Hoffmann? He's the one who runs the Steak and Brew on Sunrise Highway, isn't he?"

"Well, I don't know how to broach this delicately, but an elderly gentleman in my congregation, Mr. Joseph Henkin, told me something shocking last night. Henkin is a survivor of the Holocaust in Europe, and he claims that Heinrich Hoffmann is a former Nazi officer that he knew by a different name. Something strange may really be going on."

"You realize, Rabbi, that you are opening a can of worms with an accusation like that?" asked Grady. "This Heinrich Hoffmann is one of the biggest contributors to the Police Benevolent Association. The whole police force has an open invitation to free meals at his restaurant at any time. I've met him, and he seems concerned and decent, just a Belwyn businessman."

"What about his White America Party? Aren't you heading a department to combat bigotry and prejudice?" asked the rabbi.

"People can have their *opinions,* so long as they don't commit any crimes. We can't arrest people just for being bigots."

"But your department was *formed* to combat this kind of bigotry!" the rabbi insisted.

"I need proof. What you just told me is too serious just to pursue lightly. I'll try to look into it from my end, but so far it's just conjecture and imagination."

Inspector Grady stood up. It was a sign that the interview was over. Rabbi Rosen and the Lazarus children left his office and closed the door behind them.

They did not know that Inspector Grady reached for the telephone as they were walking down the stairs. Grady punched the numbers out on the telephone and waited for an answer. "Hello? Mr. Hoffmann? He's not in? I'll call back later."

"Well, let's get more proof," said Terri, as the four walked back down Seaville Avenue.

"Yes," said Robert. "Then the police will handle it."

"I'm glad this new task force was formed," added the rabbi. "It's long overdue."

"I think we got a runaround," said Jeff. "The police won't do anything."

"I forgot to report about the brick!" said the rabbi, striking his forehead with the heel of his right hand.

They walked past a poster in a store window. It advertised a lecture on the history of the Arabs of Palestine to be held next Saturday evening in the Rhine Room of the Bavarian Steak and Brew.

They were so busy talking, they didn't even notice it.

15

The Accident

Saturday Afternoon. 4:30 P.M.

Mordecai and Dovid played on the floor at the foot of the bed. It was some little boy's game for *Shabbos,* perhaps with toy men and horses, Henkin couldn't tell. Mordecai and Dovid were cheerful little boys in ragged clothing with clotted, bloody circles on their foreheads.

"I'm going to be a doctor when I grow up," Mordecai was telling Dovid.

Hannah came into the bedroom and leaned over Henkin's bed. She had no face.

"Time to get up for *shul,* my love. Time to get up or you'll be late. Don't be late, my love. Don't be late, after all these years."

Henkin roused himself and shouted suddenly and out loud, "He's in Belwyn! I saw! Not for our sake, but for God's justice, he will pay for his crimes! I saw him, my dearest. I saw him!"

He heard himself yelling. He looked around.

He was alone in the bedroom on Seaville Avenue.

Henkin glanced over at the small electric alarm clock on the night table beside the bed. 4:30 P.M. It was time to get up and go back to the synagogue for the Sabbath afternoon *minyan.* The schedule of services at the Belwyn Jewish Center punctuated Henkin's life with regularity.

Henkin put on his *Shabbos* suit. He wondered how the children and the rabbi had fared at the police station. Then, to his image in the bureau-top mirror, he said, "How did I get to be such an old man? Why me? There were so many who were more worthy than I."

After locking the front door of the Lazarus house from the outside, Henkin began his slow walk up Seaville.

Rabbi Rosen and the Lazarus children were approaching the synagogue along Seaville Avenue from the opposite direction. They were still about two blocks away.

"There must be more we can do," said Jeff. "I hate just doing nothing."

"We *are* doing something, Jeff," answered the rabbi. "We set in motion a legal process with the police. We publicized the problem in the press. I hope, at least, we made the congregation aware of the importance of the issue."

"It doesn't seem enough," countered Jeff. "We should get together and really fight back. Do unto them what they did to us. Know what I mean?"

"Jeff, we must let the police handle this. That's why there are laws and police and courts. Even in a place where there are no humans, we must try to behave like humans. How much more so, when we live in a place where there *are* good people and good laws."

Robert added, "Our Dad will be home tomorrow evening. He can be a big help once he hears what's happened, especially for Henkin. I know he'll help."

The rabbi nodded in agreement. "I was thinking about your father, myself. He is active on the Belwyn Jewish Community Council. He's always been a strong voice for what's important and what's right. And I'm certain that he can help us."

"And I'm going to write my first article about it for our school newspaper, after Shabbat, of course," mentioned Terri. "My journalism club teacher is against the article, though, and I don't understand why. She's Jewish."

The rabbi thought for a moment, then offered his best guess. "A lot of Jews are just uncomfortable when they are forced to face their own Jewishness." He looked ahead, down the street. "Look, there's Henkin crossing the street for the *shul*. Old Faithful. He never misses a service."

Henkin was cursing Lieutenant Kurt Hammerstein in his mind. He knew, in the deep recesses of his heart, that Kurt Hammerstein and Heinrich Hoffmann were one and the same. But, how to prove it? How to make anyone care after all these years?

Henkin stepped off the curb.

Suddenly, the dented, late-model sedan that had been left on the synagogue parking lot from Wednesday to Friday squealed with the sound of rubber pealing. It came from a dead stop not twenty feet away from the preoccupied Henkin, plummeting at ever-increasing speed. There were four teenage boys inside.

Horrified and helpless, the rabbi and the three Lazarus kids could see what was about to happen.

The car lurched and screeched. It caught Henkin on its front bumper like a charging bull. Henkin was tossed back to the grass strip at curbside like a crumpled piece of paper blown by a gust of wind. The sedan lurched again and sped down Seaville Avenue, jumping the red traffic light at the first intersection. Officer Oates, who happened to be sitting at the adjacent corner in his squad car, hoping to pick up some traffic violators on a lazy Saturday afternoon at the start of his duty, flashed his lights and sounded his siren and took off in hot pursuit.

Rabbi Rosen and the Lazarus trio ran at full speed to where Henkin was lying on his back, his arms spread like a soaring bird. His glasses were gone. His hat still rolled down the street like a dropped penny.

The rabbi commanded, "Stay with him. But *don't* touch him. I'm going inside the *shul* to call an ambulance."

Henkin opened his eyes and groaned. "It's *Shabbos*. I won't allow it."

"Not where there's a danger to life concerned," muttered the rabbi, as he dashed across to the side door of the synagogue. As he opened the parking lot entrance, he flashed again on the black painted slogan, "Kill the Jews!"

Mrs. Anderson stood in the doorway of her little Cape Cod cottage. She came to the door when she heard the screech and the thud. Now she watched the girl and the two boys huddle around the old man lying on the sidewalk. Mrs. Anderson knit her brow. She looked concerned.

16
An Eye for an Eye

Sunday morning. 1:30 A.M.

Jeff lay in bed, under the covers, fully clothed. His back-lighted digital clock radio told him that it was very late. Or very early. One thirty in the morning.

"I sure hope Robbie and Terri are fast asleep," he thought.

The children and the rabbi had stayed with Henkin at the hospital through the long ordeal in the emergency ward, and after, when Henkin was assigned a room. Henkin had been pretty lucky. He was very bruised and sore. But, like a miracle, the only broken bone was in his left forearm. It would take a while to heal at his age, but the doctor had said it *would* heal. Henkin had to stay in the hospital a few days, but mostly for observation.

The rabbi's wife had driven to the hospital and taken them all home about ten that night. Exhausted, Terri and Robert went right to bed. Dad was expected at the airport around three o'clock Sunday afternoon. They had so much to tell him to bring him up-to-date on events in Belwyn since last Wednesday night.

Jeff hoped his siblings were asleep because he had made some plans of his own.

He threw off the covers and got down on all fours on the carpeted floor by the bed. He searched in the dark, by feel, for his Puma all-court sneakers. Finding them, he slipped them on and groped in the dark for his desk chair on which he had left his black pullover sweatshirt. Sweatshirt on, he sneaked out of the bedroom to the hallway. There were no lights from under Robert or Terri's doors.

"So far, so good. Now to get out of the house without waking anyone." Jeff put his hand in his pants pocket to make sure he had his house key. "Good. It's here. I hope the other guys got out of their houses, all right."

Jeff walked up Seaville Avenue toward the parking lot of the Belwyn Jewish Center.

A slow-moving car, one of the community civilian patrol cars, turned from a side street onto Seaville. Jeff dived into the shadows, beyond the light of a street lamp, behind a border clump of azalea bushes on the nearest lawn.

The car passed and continued down Seaville, making a right turn onto another side street.

Jeff kept to the shadows until he reached the parking lot. No lights were on in the synagogue or the lot. Still, Jeff could make out the big swastika by the light of the street lamps.

"Ps-s-s-st, Jeff!" He heard a loud whisper.

Turning in the direction of the sound, Jeff discerned two boys standing in a dark corner of the empty lot. They were both slightly older than Jeff. He knew them from the congregation. They were Terri's age and went to the high school. Jeff had telephoned the taller one very secretly earlier that night after returning home from the hospital. He had arranged this meeting. He was feeling angry, even now.

All he really knew about these boys was they were members of the Hebrew Defenders, a Jewish organization that trained kids to fight back. They were guys who wouldn't take persecution lying down.

"Do you have the can of spray paint?" asked Jeff in an undertone.

"Does a plumber go out without a monkey wrench?" answered Neal, the taller boy.

"What do we do next? I've never done anything like this before," whispered Jeff.

"We make sure the coast is clear. We work fast. Then we run like hell. Nothing to it. Ready?"

Jeff swallowed hard. "Ready."

No cars were in sight.

The three boys ran across Seaville Avenue and up the walk leading to the Cape Cod cottage.

Neal handed Jeff the can of spray paint. It hissed for long minutes about six inches away from the storm door. Then the boys ran. The two Hebrew Defenders ran west and Jeff ran east down Seaville Avenue.

Jeff paused to toss the paint can down a sewer just as a battered old pickup truck came down the avenue. The headlamps of the truck illuminated Jeff, and the truck came to a stop.

Inside, wearing a cowboy hat, was Johnny, custodian of the Belwyn Jewish Center.

"Jeff Lazarus! What are you doing out at this time of night. What did you just throw down that sewer? Are you in some kind of trouble?"

Jeff didn't know what to say.

Johnny said, "Whatever it is, let me get you home, *pronto!* Get in." He swung open the passenger door of the pickup. Jeff got in. The truck made a U-turn on Seaville Avenue.

Johnny dropped Jeff off in front of the Lazarus house. "Whatever you're up to, I didn't see you tonight," said Johnny. "But you're a kid with a conscience, Jeff. If you did something wrong, you'll make it right."

Johnny waited for Jeff to get back into his house.

The truck made another U-turn and rattled up the avenue toward the custodian's house that stood behind the Jewish Center.

Had Johnny noticed, he might have seen, even in the dark, on the storm door of the Anderson home across from the synagogue parking lot, a spray-painted Star of David and the slogan, "Never Again!"

Back down Seaville Avenue, Jeff went to bed with his conscience.

17
Bikkur Holim

Sunday Morning. 7:30 A.M.

A pretty, blonde nurse in her mid-twenties gently nudged Henkin awake very early Sunday morning. A hypodermic needle was in her right hand.

Henkin opened his eyes and looked up with a start. The room was unfamiliar, a hospital room. Henkin was lying in a hospital bed!

Confused, Henkin focussed with horror on the source of the professional, pleasant voice. A blonde young woman with a hypodermic needle!

"It's just a pain killer, Mr. Henkin," she smiled.

Henkin cringed.

"No needles! No needles! I can still work. Ask anyone. The uniform is nearly finished. No needles. Let me just go back to the factory. You'll see." He was rattling on in German. The nurse didn't understand a word.

She patted Henkin's forehead with her left hand. Then, very quickly, she rubbed alcohol with a cotton puff on a spot on Henkin's right arm and smoothly administered the injection.

"You'll be feeling better in a few minutes. You had a nasty accident, yesterday. But, you'll be fine. Have a nice day. Breakfast will be coming up soon. On your chart it says you get the kosher diet. Ring, if you have any problems."

She left the room.

Slowly, Henkin remembered it all. He was in the Belwyn Community Hospital. His left arm was in a plaster cast. The only other bed in the room was empty, raised, and sheetless.

Henkin looked at the one window on the side of the room close by his bed. It was light outside. There was that special softness of early morning light.

"What time is it?" Henkin mused out loud, to no one in particular. "She said breakfast soon. *Gott in himmel!* I'll miss *minyan!* How can I daven?"

As if on cue, Rabbi Rosen entered the room.

"I brought your *tallis, tefillin,* and *siddur* over from the closet in the chapel. I figured you'd be wanting them by now. It's 7:30 in the morning. I can stay a while, until I have to get back to the *shul* for *minyan* myself. How do you feel?"

"How should I feel? I feel lousy. I hurt all over, even though they gave me a pain killer."

"It could have been worse. Thank God, you're still with us to complain."

"Boruch Ha-Shem. Did they catch the Nazis who did this?"

"I haven't heard yet. I'll go over to the precinct station after *minyan."*

Then Rabbi Rosen asked in his cheerful, pastoral voice, "You feel like davening?"

"I can't stand up."

"So daven in bed."

"How can I put the *shel yad* over a cast? The strap has to touch skin. You know that, Rabbi."

"So, in cases like this, you put the *shel yad* on your right arm. It's legal."

"I can't even move my left arm enough to put my *tefillin* on."

"So? I'll help you. What do you think I'm here for?"

Rabbi Rosen cranked Henkin's bed to a sitting

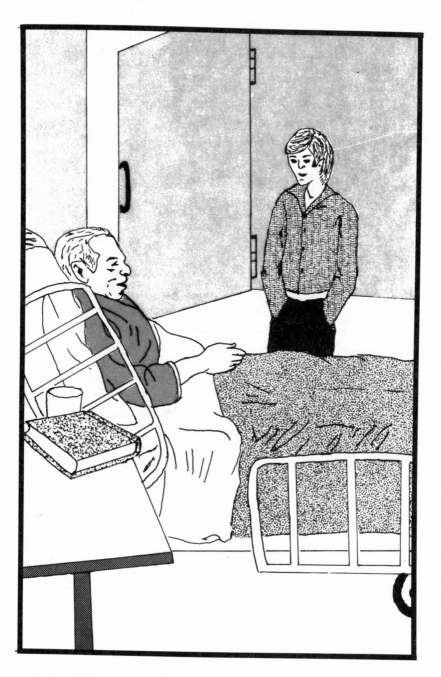

"Remember me?" he asked. "You taught me Bar Mitzvah lessons. I'm Brian Epstein."

position. He placed the *tallit* and *tefillin* on Henkin while the old man mumbled the blessings. The rabbi sat in a chair while Henkin prayed the entire morning service in bed.

When Henkin was through, the rabbi rose to help him remove his religious attire.

Henkin said softly, "You American rabbis are all right."

"And it isn't even time to renew my contract," said Rabbi Rosen with a wink.

The rabbi left, wishing Henkin a *refuah shlemah*, a full recovery.

Henkin still sat upright in the bed. He liked it that way.

"*Oy*, does my body hurt," Henkin murmured out loud to himself. Then, "*Ribono shel Olam*, this is a real *agmas nefesh!* All my life, one suffering after another. So it is said, 'troubles sustain you,' but when is enough? *Genug schein*, already! Where is the quality of mercy? When the wicked spring up like grass, aren't they supposed to be destroyed forever? I know Your greatness is unsearchable, God. But maybe I am the fool who doesn't understand. Were our sins that great?"

Breakfast arrived. Henkin ate, in bed.

Henkin looked at the plastic dish, the plastic utensils, the plastic cup. Everything disposable. The kosher meal. "It seems so true to life. What nourishes and sustains us is destined to be discarded. Yet, we may be one step closer to God's ending evil. Still, in Belwyn, when grass grows, everyone has it mowed down once a week. By the next week, it has to be mowed again. Who knows? It is not our place to know."

Time went slowly.

9:00 A.M.

A teenager diffidently approached Henkin's bedside.

"Remember me?" he asked. "You taught me Bar Mitzvah lessons. I'm Brian Epstein."

Henkin really could not see well without his glasses, but he knew the name Brian Epstein well enough.

"Sure, I remember you," he said. "You're the *meshumed*."

Brian swallowed hard. He didn't understand the Yiddish word Henkin had used, but he sensed in Henkin's tone of voice that it was an insult. "What does that *mean*?"

"*Meshumed:* One who is *destroyed,* a Jew who has gone over to *shmad,* the destruction of the spirit caused by alien faiths. It means an apostate, someone who cuts himself off from his Jewish people and eats sour grapes. A good enough definition for you, *meshumed?*"

"Henkin," said Brian slowly. "I came to make a hospital visit to you. I heard about the accident. All Belwyn is talking about it now. I just had to see you, to talk to you. Please."

Henkin was worked up already.

"So, what are you going to talk about? You think you can convince *me,* Henkin, to believe in 'Yashka Pandra'? Listen, sonny. For anything you can quote me, I can quote you ten times over. You're dealing here with an expert, sonny. So, why don't you give up now?"

Brian whispered, "I didn't come to talk about Jesus. Lots of things have happened to me since Wednesday night. I'm scared a little, and confused. You were the only person I could think of that I wanted to talk to. If you want me to leave, I'll leave."

Henkin softened his heart before the troubled boy. "So, talk." he said.

"The swastika really upset me, and scared me," said Brian. "I kind of hated the Belwyn Jewish Center myself, but I saw the swastika as a threat against me, too. More than that. I saw the kids who did it. I pulled in my car just as they were finishing. They started to come towards *me*. I could feel their hatred. I knew I had to get out of there for my own good. So, I drove away as fast as I could. I was real scared. I knew they'd come and find me if I didn't keep my mouth shut. I feel so ashamed."

"Ashamed because you saved yourself?" Henkin was beginning to feel sorry for having been so quick to judge Brian. "You know something, sonny?"

"What?"

"I'm a Holocaust survivor. Sometimes I feel ashamed that I lived when so many better people lost their lives. You can learn to live with shame. Adam and Eve felt shame only *after* they knew right from wrong. Maybe one can do *teshuvah,* turning from sin, only after you feel shame."

"But, I didn't stand up as a Jew. I ran. And, then, the police suspected *me* of painting the swastika!"

"You have to admit, they had reason. They knew your car was there, in the first place. In the second place, a Jew with Jesus *mishugas* is a suspicious character even to the *goyim!*"

"I always felt Jewish. Jesus made me feel complete. By believing in Jesus, I was relieved of the burden of sins and doubt."

"You don't sound so relieved," Henkin said.

"Not since Wednesday night. I feel miserable."

"Why? Because the police came to get you?"

"No. Because the swastika on the synagogue door was meant for me as well as you. Because I am a Jew."

"A Jew for Jesus. That kind?"

"Henkin, I don't know anymore."

"Okay. We all wait for the Messiah. We all hope for better times. In history, we hoped so hard that a few times we thought the Messiah had arrived. Jesus was not the first, nor the last that Jews put their hopes in. The *goyim* made him into a god. But did the world change? Is this the better world?"

"No. At least, I don't think so."

"So?"

"I feel miserable. I want to come back into the Jewish community, I think. Do you think I can?"

"Were you baptized?"

"No. Our group talked about it for the future, but we Jews were not baptized in order to become Jews for Jesus."

"So. You weren't baptized. You were just thinking and talking crazy. A lot of Jews do that!"

"Henkin, please don't make fun of me."

"*Agmas nefesh.* Suffering. You're suffering. I'm suffering. Brian, you *are* a Jew."

"Suffering? Is that what makes a Jew?"

"No. Everyone suffers. But recognizing and sharing the suffering—and sharing the joys, too—as a community, as a *mispocheh,* a family. It is sharing Torah. It's our holy days. It's our people, our *Eretz Yisroel,* our synagogue. It is the one, true God. But, Brian, I don't have to tell you this. You know."

"Can—can I come back?"

"You ask *me?* What am *I?* A substitute Jesus? Sonny, you *already* came back."

"Thank you, Henkin."

"*Oy, Gottenu.* Listen, *boychik.* Can you still read Torah? You *could* back then for your Bar Mitzvah ceremony."

"Yes. I read Torah sometimes at the Jews for Jesus synagogue."

"Forget *where!* You can *lein,* right?"

"Yes, I can chant from the Torah."

"So. It looks like I'm going to be laid up for a while. Until I get better, the Belwyn Jewish Center will need someone to read Torah at the weekday *minyan.* Why don't *you* do it? I'll set it straight with the rabbi." Henkin looked at Brian. "But, no Jesus funny business, understand?"

"Yes. Yes, Henkin. I want to do it."

"*A gezint af dein Yiddische kopf.*"

"What's that mean?"

"It means you'll do well."

Brian got up to leave. He took Henkin's right hand.

Henkin muttered to himself, *"Yisroel, af al pi she-hattah, Yisroel."*

"Henkin, what does *that* mean?"

Henkin smiled. "It means that a Jew is still a Jew, even if he's been acting like a horse's behind."

"Henkin," said Brian, a sad smile on his face, "I'm going down to the police station right now and give them a description of the kids I saw painting the swastika on the synagogue door. I even know the name of one of them, Keith Anderson."

"Thank you, young man. It will help tremendously in solving this case, if you will give us a statement. Wait a moment, and I'll take you down to the station in my car." It was Inspector Grady. He walked in through the doorway and came over to Brian and Henkin.

"I just spoke with Rabbi Rosen, then came over to speak with you, Mr. Henkin," the inspector went on. "We've had quite a night at the precinct station, all because of your little mishap."

"You caught the hoodlums who ran me down?" asked Henkin, choosing purposely not to use the word "Nazis."

"They were apprehended almost immediately after the accident by Officer Oates who was on patrol nearby. He had to chase them through two towns before he stopped them! Your Rabbi Rosen had the foresight to call the station and report that it was Hoffmann's car right after he called for the ambulance. Oates got the radio report while he was in pursuit and he brought the kids to the station."

"And, so?"

"Then the fun began. Hoffmann had reported his

car stolen. When the kids heard *that,* they broke down and accused Hoffmann of *ordering* them to run you down. They confessed to working for Hoffmann's White America Party. They even confessed to painting the swastika on the synagogue. Hoffmann has been brought in for questioning. The place is a *circus* with accusations and counter-accusations. I came to see you because *your* statement will be important."

"So you believe me that Heinrich Hoffmann is really Kurt Hammerstein?"

"First things first. Boy, was *I* wrong about that man. He's in a lot of trouble just over the hit-and-run, let alone the swastika. You can worry about what his real name is *later.*"

"It's important to *me.*"

"Look, I'm going to send someone over in a little while. You can dictate your statement. Meanwhile, I'll take young Epstein with me to the station and get his statement."

"Do me just one favor before you go, Inspector?"

"What is it, Mr. Henkin?"

Henkin turned his eyes toward the telephone by his hospital bed. "Dial me a number I'll give you. I want to tell the Lazarus kids."

18

Father Knows Best

Sunday Afternoon. 3:00 P.M.

"Where's Jeff?" shouted Terri, annoyed, to Robert who was already walking toward the arrivals corridor beyond the airport terminal lounge.

"He said he was going to buy a Hershey bar," Robert shouted back.

"Typical. Typical. Dad's been away for a week. We couldn't wait to tell him everything that's happened in Belwyn while he was gone. And at the moment Dad's arriving, Jeff has to be a nerd and run off looking for chocolate bars!"

"Aw, Terri. Relax. Jeff'll be here in a minute. Look! There's Dad! *Dad!*"

Edmund Lazarus smiled when he saw Terri and Robert. He was an athletic man of forty-six, medium height, a graying handlebar moustache complementing the tweed of his Irish country hat. His bent briar pipe and tan trenchcoat completed the picture, making him quite a romantic figure, something unusual among diamond merchants.

"Hi, kids." He hugged Robert and Terri as he pulled them along towards the lobby. "Where's Jeff?"

"Oh, the little twerp went looking for chocolate

bars. I *told* him you'd be in any second," said Terri. "Dad, I'm so glad you're home."

"So am I. So am I," responded Mr. Lazarus. He did not pursue it further, but seemed to be remembering something about this trip that he wasn't planning to share with them. "Okay, then, let's go looking for the chocolate freak, then go down and get my luggage. I brought you all some souvenirs from Antwerp."

"Dad, we have a million things to tell you about Belwyn and what happened to the Temple. And Henkin's in the hospital," spluttered Robert in rapid order.

"What?"

Then they discovered Jeff, sitting on a plastic lobby chair, eating a half-melted chocolate bar.

"Hi, Dad," he said, looking up. "Can I talk to you when we get home?" Jeff saw Terri's face fill with disapproval. He added, "Privately?"

"Sure. What's going on?"

Robert and Terri filled their father in on everything during the car ride from the airport to their home. Jeff was peculiarly silent.

At home, Edmund Lazarus showered and shaved. He put on a turtleneck sweater, fresh slacks, and a tweed sportcoat. Feeling refreshed, he joined the three young Lazaruses in the television room. The T.V. was on, but no one was really watching.

Robert said, "Boy, we thought that after your flight, you would want to sack out totally until tomorrow. We were going to make dinner for ourselves."

"Nothing doing. First of all, we're going to see Henkin at the hospital. Then we'll stop down at Belwyn Harbor and eat at Ron's Kosher Deli."

"I'm not very hungry," said Jeff. "Mind if I don't go?"

"Jeff, are you feeling okay?" his father asked.

"He's been acting weird all day," Terri put in.

"Aren't you even glad to see your father home after a week, you little crud?"

"I am," Jeff insisted. "Dad, can we have that private talk, later?"

"Sure, but come with us now. We're going as a *family*. I haven't seen you guys all week. I really missed you three."

"You didn't call once," chided Terri.

"I couldn't. Believe me." Then, as though to change the subject, Edmund Lazarus said, "So let's go, already."

Rabbi Rosen was sitting by Henkin's hospital bed, talking, when the Lazarus family came in.

"I'm willing to take a chance with the Epstein kid, provided he really has *harata*, regrets, as you say."

"Let him read Torah for the *minyonim*, at least, Rabbi. My instinct tells me he's a sincere *baal teshuvah*, a real returnee. It's a time to be *mekarev*, you know."

"I trust you, Henkin. We'll give him a chance. I'll call him tonight about tomorrow morning's reading."

"Good. And, thank you, Rav Rosen."

"You've never called me a *rav* before."

"This week, you've earned it," smiled Henkin.

"I'll be leaving soon. My family is invited to dinner at the Williams' family. Remember that tall young man who made up the minyan Friday night?"

"The Falasha? Have a good time."

"I don't know that he's a Falasha, Henkin. Not all black Jews are from Ethiopia. But he surely is a Jew."

Edmund Lazarus broke into the conversation.

"Hello, Rabbi Rosen. And, Henkin ... what did you do to yourself?"

"Mr. Lazarus. *Baruch ha-ba*. Welcome home. We've had a busy week here in Belwyn. Did the kids tell you?" said the young rabbi.

"They sure did. Henkin, how do you feel?"

"Rotten. But, what's the use to complain?"

"Mr. Lazarus, you have a lot of connections," Rabbi Rosen continued. "Do you know anyone who can advise us whether we have a further case against this Heinrich Hoffmann as an ex-Nazi?"

"Kurt Hammerstein," corrected Henkin.

"I'll make a phone call in the morning to a friend of mine who works for the Office of Special Investigation at the U.S. Department of Justice. We can at least begin to look into it. It's a long process, anyway, even if we find out that Hoffmann lied to gain entry to this country. But, we'll start working on it."

"Thanks. I have to go now, so please excuse me." Rabbi Rosen shook hands all around.

"So, *nu,* tell me, Edmund, what's new in Antwerp?" asked Henkin after the rabbi was gone.

"There's a lot of anti-Semitism and anti-Israel feeling in Europe just now."

"So what else is new?"

"It's really felt—in the press, on television. Belgium is dependent on Arab oil, like most countries in Europe. There are signs of much petro-dollar investment all over. It's definitely a touchy period for Jews. Especially, with the world economy so shaky."

"Edmund, it's an old story. How was your trip otherwise?"

"I accomplished what I had to. Enough said."

"You can help with our situation here?" asked Henkin.

"I'll do what I can. It won't be easy. Remember, Hoffmann by now is an old man. Many people react negatively to our pressing these old cases. They would rather let bygones be bygones after so many years."

"I know. Turn the other cheek. Only the *Jews* are expected to behave the way the Christians preach."

"I'll do what I can, Henkin. I promise you."

"Edmund, I'm an old man, too. But these memories are as fresh as today."

"I'll do what I can. Look, we'll stop back tomorrow. I'm taking the kids out to dinner."

8:00 P.M.

Back home from the kosher deli, Terri went up to her room and wrote her story for the school newspaper. She tried to write it as Henkin would tell it. Then she gave it the title, "The Swastika on the Synagogue Door." Robert was on the phone in the kitchen with Lauryn for a long time. Lauryn had called just after the Lazarus family walked in the door of their home. Jeff and Mr. Lazarus, sitting in the living room, could sometimes hear small snatches of Robert's conversation.

"So you had a terrible time this weekend . . . Sure, I was hurt . . . Okay . . . I still do want to go out with you . . . I, I like you, Lauryn."

Robert looked up into the living room. He put the telephone receiver on the table and went to close the door to the kitchen.

Jeff looked at his father.

"Something is bothering you, Jeff. Go ahead, now, tell me what it is and how I can help."

"I did a terrible thing," Jeff said. "I'm ashamed even to tell you. And, I'm scared to do anything about it."

"You don't have to tell me if you don't want to. As long as you think you can make it right."

"No. I have to tell. It's a big thing, and I don't know if I can make it right. I could be in a lot of trouble."

"Well, start at the beginning and let's see."

"Dad, this Keith Anderson kid was picking on me at school. He's one of the kids who was arrested for running Henkin down with the car."

"And . . ."

"Well, I kind of thought he was involved in the whole swastika business, even before we had real proof. And, I didn't think the police would ever do anything."

"I see."

"There's more. I kinda painted a Jewish star on his family's aluminum door, sorta to give him back what he did to us."

"Oh."

"It wasn't right. It kinda makes me the *same* as him. You see what I mean?"

"What do you think you should do?"

"I want to confess. But I'm scared that I'll be arrested and have a police record and never get into college, or whatever."

"What if we call the Andersons? Do you think you can clean the door?"

"I don't know. That spray paint is pretty powerful. I have some money saved. How much does an aluminum door cost?"

"I guess about a hundred dollars, or so. It's been a long time since I went door shopping."

"I was saving to get a bunch of new videogames. I have nearly eighty dollars in my savings account."

"I suppose I could advance you the rest, if it costs more."

"Dad, I'm scared. Keith has been arrested. If I call them about this, they could get me arrested, too—to even the score. They must really hate Jews, anyway."

"It seems to me that you've thought out the possibilities. What do you think you should do?"

"I can't live with it like it is now. I should confess and apologize to them and get them a new door."

"Well, we don't know what will happen unless we try to do what we think is right."

"Dad, could you call for me?"

"I think we'd better go in person."

8:45 P.M.

Jeff stood beside his father on the doorstep. He had just told Mrs. Anderson. "I want to pay for the door, if we can't get the paint off," he added.

Mrs. Anderson asked the two to come into her living room. Father and son sat together on the sofa by the bay window. Mrs. Anderson sat on an easy chair.

She spoke first to Mr. Lazarus. "I was angry at you Jews when my son was arrested. And, when I discovered that star on my front door this morning, I called the police. Then I thought, it's just God's way of punishing me. A cross to bear for Keith's behavior lately. In my heart, I know he's not an easy child.

"My husband walked out on us three years ago. It's not easy raising a boy without his father. I guess the truth is, I've failed.

"We've lived here across from the synagogue ever since Keith was born. We never had a bad word to say about the Jewish people in all that time. I don't know how he got so involved in that group. Now, I'm worried sick. How is that poor old man doing?"

"Henkin? The doctors say he'll be fine," said Mr. Lazarus. "He's a tough old bird."

"Thank God. And what will happen to Keith?"

"I don't know," Edmund answered. He felt empathy with her, parent to parent.

"Oh, the door is the least of my problems now."

"I really have the money for a new one," said Jeff. "I'm really sorry for what I did."

"I heard that Keith was picking on you in school. He bragged about locking you in your locker. I'm sorry about that, too. I wish I had known sooner. Maybe all this could have been avoided. I had a feeling something was wrong since Wednesday night when he stayed out late with his friends."

"Could I pay for a new door?" asked Jeff.

"I suppose so," Mrs. Anderson answered, distracted.

She started crying. "We'll need a lawyer. I don't have much money. Could you help me find a lawyer who will understand? Lots of Jews are lawyers. Do you think a Jewish lawyer would defend Keith after what he did?"

Mr. Lazarus took a deep breath. "I know some lawyers. I'll have one get in touch with you tomorrow. Still, a lot depends on Keith himself, and how the judge assesses him."

"I'd really be grateful for any help, Mr. Lazarus. I don't know where to turn." She looked at Jeff. "The star on my door was my cross to bear. I forgive you. Please forgive Keith and me."

Jeff said, "I'll pay for a new door."

Mrs. Anderson nodded.

She looked again at Edmund Lazarus.

"Please help my son."

Edmund Lazarus looked sideways at Jeff. To Mrs. Anderson, he said, "I'll do what I can."

19
Another Day

Monday Afternoon.

Terri and Mary Beth went right up to Terri's bedroom and threw their schoolbooks down on the canopy bed. It had been a long school day. Terri flipped through her record collection until she found a Pink Floyd.

With the L.P. silently spinning inside the plastic dust cover of the turntable, and the music loudly flowing from the two huge stereo speakers, no one except Terri and Mary Beth could possibly hear what was being said.

Mary Beth was sitting on the floor at the foot of Terri's bed. "Terri, I think it's just *excellent* that Mr. Rosetti assigned Christine and her friends to a tutorial with *you* in biology! That'll really show them."

"Oh, just *super*," said Terri, sarcastically.

"Why, I think it's quite an honor for you! You'll be good for them. They'll probably even pass biology with your help."

"Sure. How to win friends and influence people."

"Gee, aren't you the cheerful one. Are we gonna be subject to another Terri mood? In that case, I'll turn up the music."

"Okay, I'm sorry. I'm still ticked at Ms. Feingold.

She *rejected* my story on the swastika. She still thinks it has no place in the Belwyn High *Blast*."

"So? Too bad for her."

"Shut up. I've got an idea. Turn off the stereo a minute, will you?"

"Sure."

Terri reached for the trimline phone on her night table. She dialed a number after finding it in the little Nassau directory she kept in her table drawer.

Mary Beth watched as Terri's face changed from one of serious business to a broad grin.

Terri hung up the phone and hugged Mary Beth. "I just called *Newsday*. They're interested in my article! Let's find an envelope so I can mail it right away!"

"Oh, *wow!*" said Mary Beth.

Robert and Jeff came into the room.

"You'll never guess who read the Torah at *minyan* this morning. *Brian Epstein!* He was pretty good at it, too," Robert said.

Jeff added, "It's a real metamorphosis, just like your Rana *pipiens!*"

Terri's smile evaporated. To Jeff she said, "Don't talk to me about *biology,* understand?"

Jeff shrugged his shoulders. Robert and Mary Beth laughed.

The telephone rang. Terri picked it up. There was a nervous voice at the other end.

"Terri?"

"This is Terri."

"Hi."

"Hi. Who *is* this?"

"Um, Brian."

"*Which* Brian?"

"Brian Epstein."

"Oh. Can I help you? You want to speak to Robbie?"

"Uh, no. I want to speak, uh, with you."

"Oh."

"I was wondering, well, maybe if you aren't doing anything Saturday, Saturday night, I mean, maybe, you might, uh, like to go out with me. Okay?"

Terri said, "No."

She hung up the phone and told Robert and Jeff that she was sending her article about the swastika to *Newsday*.

At the Belwyn Jewish Center, Rabbi Rosen was on the telephone with Edmund Lazarus.

"What did you find out?" asked the rabbi.

"As I suspected, we have a long process ahead of us, if we want to go for Hoffmann's deportation to Poland to face war crimes charges. A source of mine in the Justice Department confirmed Henkin's suspicion that he was really Kurt Hammerstein. They have a file on ex-Nazis in Special Investigations. But there's a fly in the ointment. It seems he did some intelligence work for the U.S. Army right after the war, against the Russians. That's how he got into this country with a new name. We've got a struggle ahead of us if we want to go beyond the charges against him for Henkin's 'accident.' "

"Well, let's leave it up to Henkin. I was planning on seeing him in the hospital in a little while, anyway."

"I'll be there with the kids to see him before dinner. What's the latest with the teenagers who were in the car?"

"They're being held until bail can be set. Probably some time today. But they're in real trouble. We'll still press charges."

"I see. Look, I'll get back to you. I'm expecting a call from Zurich, Switzerland."

"Goodbye, and thanks, Mr. Lazarus, for whatever you can do."

"It's a long road ahead, Rabbi, but at least you've brought Hoffmann's political activities and his anti-Semitism out into the open."

"At least. *Shalom.*"

Rabbi Rosen walked slowly out the side door of the synagogue. By so doing, he interrupted for a moment Johnny the custodian who was busy working on the outside of the door.

Johnny was nearly finished sanding the swastika off. A can of white paint and a paint brush were by his feet on the sidewalk.

The rabbi said, "It's almost time for the Hebrew school kids to be coming."

Johnny smiled. "I'll finish sanding, but I won't paint until tomorrow. That way, it'll be dry before the kids can get their hands on it."

The rabbi smiled. "Okay. Take a breather. Paint tomorrow. I'll see you. I'm going to drop over to see Henkin at the hospital.

The rabbi crossed the little street and walked over to his 1966 black Nova on the parking lot. His gaze absent-mindedly shifted across Seaville Avenue.

The Star of David was still on the Andersons' front door.

So were the words, "Never Again!"